Wrapping her arm around the front of his chest, she heaved him into her as she backed up the ladder leading to the dock rung by rung. At the top, she fell, taking his weight fully, but she couldn't stop.

She maneuvered out from under him. Centering the base of her palms under his sternum, she interlaced her fingers and administered compressions. "One, two, three, four..."

No response. Counting off again, she repeated the compression and filled his lungs. "Come on, Nicholas. Breathe!"

His chest jerked under her hands, and water spewed from his mouth as she rolled him onto his side. Nicholas's groan filled her ears, and relief washed through her. He was alive. He was going to make it.

"It's okay. I'm here. I'm going to get help, okay? Just stay with me, Nicholas. Stay with me."

"Hello, Dr. Flood," an unfamiliar voice said from behind.

Nicholas's hand pressed against hers, but she couldn't move, couldn't think.

The dark outline of her attacker blurred as he positioned himself over her. "I've been waiting for you."

PROFILING A KILLER

NICHOLE SEVERN

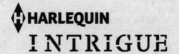

To Nana:

You always believed in my writing. I hope I've made you proud.

Special thanks and acknowledgment are given to Nichole Severn
for her contribution to the Behavioral Analysis Unit miniseries.

ISBN-13: 978-1-335-55517-5

Recycling programs
for this product may
not exist in your area.

Profiling a Killer

Copyright © 2021 by Harlequin Books S.A.

This edition published by arrangement with Harlequin Books S.A.

For questions and comments about the quality of this book,
please contact us at CustomerService@Harlequin.com.

Harlequin Enterprises ULC
22 Adelaide St. West, 40th Floor
Toronto, Ontario M5H 4E3, Canada
www.Harlequin.com

Printed in U.S.A.

Nichole Severn writes explosive romantic suspense with strong heroines, heroes who dare challenge them and a hell of a lot of guns. She resides with her very supportive and patient husband, as well as her demon spawn, in Utah. When she's not writing, she's constantly injuring herself running, rock climbing, practicing yoga and snowboarding. She loves hearing from readers through her website, www.nicholesevern.com, and on Facebook, @nicholesevern.

Books by Nichole Severn

Harlequin Intrigue

Profiling a Killer
Midnight Abduction

A Marshal Law Novel

The Fugitive
The Witness
The Prosecutor
The Suspect

Blackhawk Security

Rules in Blackmail
Rules in Rescue
Rules in Deceit
Rules in Defiance
Caught in the Crossfire
The Line of Duty

Visit the Author Profile page at Harlequin.com.

CAST OF CHARACTERS

Nicholas James—He's all too familiar with the MO found at the scene of a recent murder as the Behavioral Analysis Unit's resident serial crime expert. But when he realizes the killer left a map to the body for the victim's sister, the ME who helped put the X Marks the Spot Killer away, Nicholas knows it'll take more than past experience to stop this new evolution of murders from making her the next victim.

Aubrey Flood—The medical examiner has seen it all, but the sudden discovery of her younger sister's body throws everything she's worked for into question. Determined to help catch the killer, she comes face-to-face with the FBI agent she hasn't been able to forget since working the X Marks the Spot Killer case together three years prior.

Madeline Striker—BAU's kidnapping and abduction expert.

Dashielle West—BAU's cybercrimes expert.

The X Marks the Spot Killer—Cole Presley strangled and carved x's into the cheeks of his victims before delivering maps to find his masterpieces to the women's family members. He's the inspiration behind this new string of murders, but he isn't the only one.

Prologue

Absolutely perfect.

Short brown hair, slender through the hips, with honey-brown eyes he hadn't been able to stop thinking about since the moment he'd met her. Yes. If he had to narrow down his type, Kara Flood ticked all the boxes.

The kindergarten teacher strengthened her grip on her dog's leash, and a prickling raised the hairs on the back of his neck as he pressed back into the shadows. Her footsteps in those ridiculous platform sandals echoed off the apartment building at his back. She was getting closer, close enough he noted the streetlamp's reflection off the sweat beading along her flawless neck. It was hot out tonight, humid. Hot enough hints of her perfume tickled the back of his throat as a breeze swept off the inlet. A frenzy coiled in his gut, and he breathed the combination of orange, patchouli and Turkish rose deeper. It was the only perfume she wore.

The dog, an intrusive white shepherd who'd kept him from getting to know Kara on a more intimate level, glanced his way, but he didn't move.

Nothing would stop him from having her. Nothing would stop him from showing them what he was capable of. This was *his* time. He left the cover of the alley and cut off her escape, curling gloved fingers into fists. Hesitation combined with a slight hint of fear in her expression, and a wave of anticipation flooded through him. The dog pulled back on the leash, trying to convince Kara to leave, but there was nowhere for her to run. Not from him.

"Hello, Kara. I've been waiting for you."

Chapter One

"Seattle PD received a hand-drawn map early this morning from a witness who hasn't been able to reach her sister for over twenty-four hours." Supervisory Special Agent Miguel Peters tossed a thick manila folder onto the conference table, the scrape of card stock and wood cutting off conversation. A thick five-o'clock shadow stood stark against his white button-down shirt and showcased the exhaustion under his eyes. The supervising director of the Behavioral Analysis Unit pointed to the head of the conference room. "Now we know why."

The projector flashed to life at the direction of their tech guru—Liam McDare—at the opposite end of the table. A single image filled the screen. The bright seal of the evidence bag cut off the top two inches of a crude, torn piece of lined paper with penned outlines of vague, unlabeled buildings, sidewalks, a park and a large red *X* off to one side. SSA Peters hit the remote in his hand, and the image on the projector changed. A woman—no older than twenty-five or twenty-six—sat on a commercial steel bench outside what looked like a wall of windows leading into the main floor of an apartment building. One leg crossed over the other, the victim looked as though she'd sat down to take in the sunrise from across Puget Sound to start her morning. Aside from the angry purple-and-blue strangulation marks around her neck and the red *X* carved into her right cheekbone, she'd been a strikingly beautiful woman.

"The map designated where the victim's sister could find the body." *Hell.* Special Agent Nicholas James leaned forward in his chair, a knot of dread knifing through him. No. It wasn't possible. Reaching for the folder SSA Peters had tossed in his direction, he pried it open and compared the crime scene photos to those taking up nearly an entire wall in the BAU's high-rise conference room. All the signs were there, right down to the positioning of the body. He locked his back teeth against the denial clawing up his throat without looking up. "Who is she?"

"Victim's name is Kara Flood, a kindergarten teacher who lives in the building you see behind her, and, in case you can't tell from the crime scene photos, she resembles a few victims we've come across before." SSA Peters pressed his palms onto the edge of the long conference table. "Director Branson wants this handled as quickly and as quietly as possible. We can't have the public panic. Agents James and Striker, meet your next assignment."

A kindergarten teacher? Nausea churned in Nicholas's gut. Gravity pulled the blood from his face as he memorized the woman's features.

"The X Marks the Spot Killer." Madeline Striker, the unit's kidnapping expert, unfolded her arms and set her elbows on the table. Dark, layered hair with golden highlights framed perfectly angled warm brown cheekbones. A hard light of dedication to find the missing echoed in her dark, rich eyes. Her flawless complexion made her look younger than her age, but any perp who had the guts to take advantage learned Striker had an uncanny ability to handle herself. "He chose women who were in their early to mid-twenties, single, with short brown hair, and were much smaller than him to make it easier to strangle them from behind. He was all about control, domination. She matches his profile."

Nicholas's ears rang as images of his childhood superimposed the faces of the victims from his first case assignment for the unit three years ago. He forced himself to take a deep breath, to come up with some other explanation as to why Kara Flood had been targeted, strangled and mutilated with an *X*. They'd found the killer. They'd put the bastard behind bars.

Confusion altered the clean lines of Madeline's dark eyebrows. "He hunted his victims in that same neighborhood, but Cole Presley was found guilty and sentenced to life behind bars. We need to contact the warden at Washington State Corrections to ensure Presley is still accounted for."

"We never released the details of the X Marks the Spot case to the public, and there haven't been any leaks in information as far as I can tell after the conclusion of the trial." BAU's resident cybercrimes expert, Dashiell West, tapped his hand against the table. The light from the agent's laptop cast shadows along chiseled features and thick beard growth. Two years older than Nicholas, West had more experience in the digital world, but serial cases would always default to Nicholas. Especially this one. "The only way this guy could've gotten the specifics of how the victims were killed is if he was involved in the case somehow. Maybe one of the original victims' family members? They would've been informed about manner of death."

"The X Marks the Spot Killer strangled and mutilated thirty victims over thirty years that we know of, every year on the same day. Assuming one of the victims' family members is involved, that leaves hundreds of suspects."

Only Nicholas had known the killer by a different name when he'd been a kid. Right up until he'd put the cuffs on a man he'd trusted his entire life. The bones under his knuckles threatened to break free from the calloused skin on the back of his hands. Kara Flood. He didn't know the victim or recognize her name directly, but instinct heightened all the same as he studied postmortem photos of the woman discovered this morning. He could almost see the resemblance, and a shot of warmth dumped into his veins. Dark brown hair, same shade of honey-colored eyes, possibly a similar face shape. Had the victim been related to Dr. Aubrey Flood, the medical examiner who'd performed the autopsies on the last three victims of the X Marks the Spot Killer? He scanned the file in front of him. "The sister found the body."

"Yes." The lines around SSA Peters's mouth smoothed. "According to her statement given to Seattle PD this morning, Dr. Aubrey Flood found the map taped to her door this morning, then immediately tried calling the victim. When she didn't get an answer, she followed the clues the killer had left for her. Forensics is trying to pull prints from the map and the tape, but the lab is backed up as it is. We won't have results for a few days."

"Dr. Flood was the ME in the original case.

She performed the autopsies on Presley's last three victims." Nicholas licked his suddenly dry lips as a visual of the doc replaced the violent memories in his head. Wisps of soft medium-length brown hair highlighting a creamy complexion, a honey-warm gaze that had pierced straight through him and the voice of a siren tempting him to believe in something other than the worst in people.

He'd only met the medical examiner a handful of times to discuss the initial case, but there always seemed to be a forged intimacy between everyone involved in a serial investigation. Emergency responders, agents assigned to the case, the first officers on scene. Drowning in that kind of darkness brought out a need for safe human contact that even the most veteran investigators clung to, and Aubrey had been part of the team. She'd been professional, respectful and warm toward the victims under her scalpel, a miracle considering the kind of work she had to face on a daily basis as Seattle's chief examiner.

"She gave us the exact type of blade Cole Presley used to carve an *X* into each of the victims' cheeks by swabbing particles from the wounds and testing hundreds of blades. Without her insight, we never would've caught up to him. We can't discount the possibility her sister's death might be some kind of retaliation from one of his super fans."

"You think this killer might be trying to get the attention of the X Marks the Spot Killer by drawing out the medical examiner who put him away." SSA Peters centered himself in the light from the projector as the slideshow ended. The FBI seal tinted the antiterrorism expert's Cuban American skin tone blue.

"It makes sense, but I think there's more at play than we're seeing here. This is the first victim we've uncovered using a previous serial's MO, and something tells me it won't be the last." Not when Dr. Flood was quickly becoming a central element to this case. Nicholas studied the photos of the victim again. "It can't be a coincidence Kara Flood was strangled and marked after her sister became connected to the case, or that the killer delivered the map directly to Aubrey Flood's door. His target wasn't random."

Nicholas raised his attention to SSA Peters. The question was why. That was the specialty of the Behavioral Analysis Unit—to make sense of the incomprehensible, to get into the minds of humanity's worst killers to stop them from striking again. Cole Presley had strangled young women in their twenties with brown hair and marked them with an *X* to show the victims' family members where to find his treasure, his masterpieces, but Nicholas wasn't willing to risk Aubrey Flood's life in order to add to his profile of this killer. He closed the file in front of him. "He knew exactly what he was doing and whom he wanted to draw into his game."

"All right. I've got Caitlyn Yang meeting with Dr. Flood and the family now to fill them in on the investigation and explain where we go from here. Dr. Flood is one of us, and we owe her nothing less than the full support of this unit." SSA Peters straightened. "West, I need you to search through security footage from the good doctor's apartment building. There might be something there to give us an idea of when our unsub left the note so we can track his movements last night. James and Striker, take Dyson to check out the scene where the killer dumped the body. I want to know if anyone noticed our victim or her killer before she wound up in front of her apartment building."

"You got it." Nicholas pushed away from the conference table and headed for the double glass doors leading out into the main offices. Blinding hits of sunlight glimmered across Puget Sound through the floor-to-ceiling windows. Liam McDare, the tall, lanky IT tech with an easy smile, unplugged the projector from his laptop and nodded as he passed.

"Agent James, a minute," SSA Peters said from behind.

Pivoting, Nicholas let the team maneuver past him as he faced the supervisory agent. "Sir?"

"Dr. Flood specifically requested for you to work this case after your work together three years ago, but I know how close you were to Cole Presley before you discovered who he really was." SSA Peters stalked toward him, and Nicholas's defenses automatically bristled. "No one would blame you if you recused yourself from this case. It isn't every day we find out the people we trust aren't who they seem. The team is here for you. However you need."

His mind instantly snapped back to the moment he'd cuffed the man who'd taught him how to play catch, how to drive, who'd been the role model he'd needed in his life when his father hadn't been around. His next-door neighbor had turned out to be the X Marks the Spot Killer, the very same killer who'd inspired him to join the BAU. SSA Peters was right. He'd never be able to trust the mask people presented to the world, including the pretty face that'd been the key to putting Cole Presley behind bars. "It won't be a problem."

THE KING COUNTY Medical Examiner's Office had already taken possession of her sister's remains at her request, but Dr. Aubrey Flood could still see the exact position the killer had left Kara in. Low voices carried through the white noise of cars passing, the weight of Seattle PD's attention on her crushing what little oxygen she'd managed to hang on to since this morning from her lungs.

She stared at the bench where she'd found Kara this morning, knowing exactly where the map that'd been taped to her door would lead. She didn't know why she was here, didn't know what she'd intended to accomplish by coming back. Her sister had been strangled, carved up with a deep laceration in the shape of an *X* in her right cheek and left for her to find. A knot of familiarity twisted tight in her stomach. Dr. Archer Caldwell, her counterpart for the county, would've already done the preliminary examination by now with such a high-profile case, but Aubrey needed to be here. There were too many similarities between her sister's death and the first serial case she'd handled three years ago. She needed to find answers.

Wiping her damp palms down her slacks, she maneuvered through the crowd of onlookers and neighbors being kept behind the crime scene tape and flashed her credentials to the officer assigned perimeter security. "Excuse me, I'm Dr. Aubrey Flood with the Seattle Medical Examiner's Office. I was told Special Agent

Nicholas James from the Behavioral Analysis Unit would be on scene."

Nicholas James, the serial expert who'd caught Seattle's most notorious killer on his first assignment for the BAU. She hadn't interacted with him more than a few times when he'd been present for the autopsies of the X Marks the Spot Killer's victims, but he'd made one hell of an impression. If anyone could give her answers about the details of Kara's case, it would be him.

"The FBI just arrived, ma'am." He lifted the crime scene tape for her to pass, and she ducked underneath without hesitation. Pointing behind him, he set the perimeter back into place. "Agents James and Striker are setting up the command center across the street. The King County ME already claimed the body, though. They must've sent you by accident."

Not by accident. Aubrey's office wouldn't take responsibility for this case due to the conflict of interest, but she wasn't going to sit this one out, either. Kara had been disposed of for Aubrey to find. Like so many others before her. She nodded. "Thank you."

The command center was nothing more than a generic shade canopy with two folding tables, a few chairs and boxes of equipment the forensics team relied on to collect their evidence. Only there wouldn't be any. No DNA. No par-

ticulates they'd be able to identify on or around
the bench. Nothing. If her sister's death had anything to do with the X Marks the Spot Killer, the
attacker would've been too careful for that. Her
heart jerked in her chest as she walked toward
the tent. She forced herself to keep her attention
forward, not on the spot where she'd found Kara
this morning.

Sea-salted air grazed against her face and neck
as she caught sight of the federal agent she hadn't
been able to forget. Nicholas James. Gull calls
pierced through the hard beat of her pulse behind
her ears. Sweat that had nothing to do with the
rising temperatures of July in the Pacific North-
west beaded along her collarbone and slid beneath her shirt. Green-blue eyes—the same color
as Puget Sound behind her—locked on her as
though he'd sensed her approach, and a buzzing
filled her head. His mouth parted, highlighting
the thick, dirty-blond beard growth along his
jaw and upper lip. Styled, equally low-lit hair
protested the breeze coming off the water as
he maneuvered around the table under the canopy. A perfectly sculpted nose with a dent at
the bridge—presumably from a childhood injury—divided symmetrical features and deep
laugh lines she'd never had the pleasure of seeing firsthand, but she imagined smiles were few

and far between in his line of work. Just as they were in hers.

Aubrey extended her hand. "Special Agent James, you might not remember me, but I'm—"

"Dr. Flood." He took her hand, rough calluses tugging the oversensitized skin of her palms. His voice, smooth as one-hundred-year-old whiskey, slid through her and battled to calm the jagged edges of anxiety and grief tearing through her. "How could I forget? If it wasn't for you, Cole Presley would still be out there."

Her neck and face heated. He remembered her from their short interactions during the X Marks the Spot case, even with the added impersonal environment of her morgue in the basement of Harborview Medical downtown. She ducked her head to cut off eye contact long enough to get her head on straight and released his hand. This wasn't a social visit. This was a death scene, and it was taking every ounce of her being not to break down in the middle of it or in front of him. Swallowing the thickness in her mouth, she cleared her throat. "I gave you the specifics about the lacerations in the victims' cheeks and the blend of steel. You're the one who recognized the blade the killer used."

Warmth seeped from her hand as Nicholas pulled back. "Dr. Flood—"

"Aubrey." She folded her arms across her chest

as if one simple action could deflect what he was about to say to her. "You can call me Aubrey, and I know I'm not supposed to be here. I just..." Her gaze wandered to that spot, the bench where she'd found Kara staring out across the street as though her sister had been sitting there waiting for her to arrive. Her clothes had been pristine, probably the same outfit she'd worn to teach her kindergarten class yesterday. Not a single wrinkle or an askew fold. Her face had been flawlessly made up apart from the deep laceration in her cheek. The lack of blood in the wound indicated she'd already been dead when the killer had taken the blade—or whatever he'd used—to her sister's beautiful face.

Aubrey covered her mouth with one hand to hide the fact her lips trembled under the visual. She sniffed to gain her composure and refocused on the agent in front of her. The man who was going to find her sister's killer. She blinked to clear her head, but there was no amount of emotional detachment that would erase the images behind her eyes. Standing tall, she tried to keep the professionalism she used with decedents' family members after completing the autopsies assigned in her voice when all she wanted to do was fall apart. "Have you found her dog?"

"The victim owned a dog?" Nicholas hiked his suit jacket behind his hips and leveraged both hands at his belt. A shoulder holster traced the long, lean muscle of his torso and highlighted the strength under the clean white button-down shirt and tie.

"Yes." Aubrey nodded, for something to do other than sob in the middle of a crime scene. "Kara walked her white shepherd every night at 10:00 p.m. Dr. Caldwell—the King County ME—placed time of death around then. That's probably what my sister was doing before she was attacked."

"We didn't find any evidence of a dog, but we're waiting to hear from the owner of the victim's…your sister's building to gain access to her apartment." A flash of regret colored his expression. "Is it possible she left her apartment on her own last night?"

"It's possible, but that wouldn't explain why Kara was out so late." She struggled to come up with another reason her sister would've been out. "She wrestled with five-and six-year-olds all day at school, and part of her winding-down routine included walking Koko. She said it helped her sleep better."

"When was the last time you talked with your sister?" Agent James asked.

"We talk every night before she goes to bed, around 10:30 p.m. We never miss a call unless something comes up, but we always let each other know in advance so we don't assume the worst. Our parents—" She closed her eyes as a wave of dizziness threatened to rip the world straight out from under her. "*My* parents are retired, and unless we force them, they're not interested in leaving the house much anymore. We take turns looking in on them. We bring them groceries, take them for walks around the neighborhood, keep them company, and we update each other on any changes or problems we had during the day."

Her blood pressure spiked. Seattle PD had done their due diligence and reached out to Kara's next of kin, her parents, after Aubrey had discovered the body and called police, and she hadn't been there with them. The public relations liaison from the BAU—Caitlyn something—had reassured her mother and father that the investigation was moving in the right direction, but Aubrey should've been there. Her eyes burned. This wasn't another homicide that she'd be able to compartmentalize at the end of the day. This was Kara, and she didn't know how to process the fact someone she loved—someone she'd been responsible for—would be laid out on a cold examination table and dissected for evidence.

"That's when you knew something was wrong. When she didn't pick up the phone?" That brilliant gaze assessed her every move, every change in her expression, and she suddenly felt as though Nicholas James was the only person keeping her anchored to the earth.

"Yes," she said. "She didn't answer when I called, and I kept trying to get through to her, but there was no answer. I was getting ready to go by her apartment when I found the note taped to my door."

"Do you recall hearing anything odd outside your apartment last night between 10:00 p.m. and 11:00 p.m.? See anything unusual?" The intensity in his body language slid down to his hands as he reached into his jacket pocket for a notepad and pen.

"No. Nothing like that." He had to ask. He had to go over the details multiple times to ensure investigators wouldn't miss anything. She'd told all this to Seattle PD, but as the lead investigator on Kara's case, she understood he had to hear it for himself. "Agent James, I worked the X Marks the Spot Killer case, too. I'm familiar with the way Cole Presley killed his victims and left maps for their families to follow the clues to the bodies, and Kara was..."

She cleared her throat to regain some sense of control. "You don't need to wait for the building's owner to give you permission to enter Kara's apartment. I have a key." She pressed a hand against her neck, rolling her lips between her teeth, and bit down. Unpocketing her key ring from her slacks, Aubrey held it out for him. She couldn't say it, didn't want to believe, but the proof had been there on her sister's body. The truth surfaced as she studied him. "I gave you the evidence you needed to make the arrest three years ago. I think Kara might've been targeted because of me."

Chapter Two

Nicholas turned the key Dr. Flood—Aubrey— had given him and pushed inside her sister's apartment. A folding door stood partially open immediately to his right, another door leading into the space's only bathroom and laundry combination to his left. Sunlight crawled through the ceiling-to-floor window down a long hallway from the main living space. It seemed the bedroom had been sectioned off from the rest of the studio, and he moved inside to get a sense of the space.

Clean. Uncluttered. Warm and airy. He could almost imagine the woman who'd been found strangled on a street bench this morning outside this same building coming home after a long day of being at war with kindergartners to escape. Little noise came through the single window straight ahead, giving the apartment an isolated feel. His shoes echoed off the laminate flooring running lengthwise toward the back of the apartment. No television.

Kara Flood had been a woman dedicated to education, to shaping young minds for the future. He scanned the bookcases along the opposite wall of the kitchen. Tingling in the tips of his fingers urged him to feel the countless spines as he passed, but while the victim hadn't been killed in her apartment, anything here could be used as evidence during the investigation. He stopped in the middle of the floor, a sliding door cutting off access to the bedroom to his right. One couch, a coffee table. No room for entertaining or company. Kara hadn't been a host or someone who'd gone out of their way to connect with others socially.

This was a haven, everything in its proper order and place with soft, neutral tones. Turning toward the front door, he faced Agent Madeline Striker and the BAU's intern, David Dyson. Serial cases had a way of taking years off an agent's life, but Nicholas had found Dyson smart enough, focused enough and determined enough over the past few months to warrant including him in the investigation.

Both waited patiently for him to make his assessment, but it wasn't his team or Aubrey Flood he imagined walking down the hallway. Kara Flood's translucent outline—his interpretation of her—didn't look his way as she walked past him. He followed her every move as she glided through the space and into the kitchen. Setting her purse on the left end of the kitchen counter, she smiled as she greeted the white shepherd Aubrey had described. Retreating here from reality every day once she was finished teaching class, the victim would've been relaxed. At home. Happy.

"You want to work serial cases for the unit, Dyson? Tell me what you see." Nicholas spotted a photograph—of the victim and the missing canine in a grassy area, a park—and envisioned the sound of the dog's nails scratching on the laminate, his tail out of control in greeting. The dog's kennel was clean, filled with drinking water and a handful of dry dog food.

"Yeah, okay." At only twenty-four, David Dyson had thrived at the top of his class, graduating with his doctorate in psychology long before his peers. As the youngest prospect for the BAU, the intern had proven himself a valuable asset and eager to learn anything he could from Nicholas in the six months he'd been assigned to the unit. Chestnut skin lightened in the rays of sunlight coming through the windows as Dyson scanned the victim's personal space, took in the layout, how Kara Flood had organized her belongings. "No dirty dishes in the sink, bed made, laundry folded and put away. From a cursory search, I'd peg Kara Flood as routine, someone who would feel off throughout the day if things weren't done in a specific order by a certain time. According to Dr. Flood, the victim walked the dog every night at ten as part of her evening routine, which raises the question of where is the dog now?"

"Very good." Nicholas turned back to the space.

"I'm sorry, but how does any of this determine who killed Kara?" Aubrey asked.

"Agent James is a psychological profiler." The weight of Madeline Striker's attention weighed between his shoulder blades, but he didn't have the concentration to confirm. "The best way for him and Dyson to get a sense of a killer is to find out what it was about the victims that attracted them."

Nicholas's heart beat hard behind his rib cage. There was something here he was missing. Something Kara Flood wouldn't have told her sister about. Something that might've gotten her killed, but he wasn't seeing it. Not yet. "Did Kara spend time with friends? A boyfriend? Anyone she might not have wanted you or your parents to know about?"

"What? No. She would've told me if she was seeing anyone. We didn't keep secrets from each other." Aubrey wrung her hands together, most likely battling a hint of shame she'd let his team inside her sister's home. But if they were going to find the person who'd killed Kara Flood, they needed to know everything about the victim. "As for friends, she has the occasional meetup for coffee, but for the most part, Kara was an introvert. She taught school, then she came home and read."

The victim's belongings had been recovered with her body. Jewelry, purse—untouched as far as the first responders had been able to tell. Whoever attacked Kara Flood hadn't carved an X into her cheek out of anger or hatred. They hadn't been motivated by financial gain. Her death had been methodical, as though killing her had been the first logical step as part of a larger plan.

"Your sister made a kindergarten teacher's salary, but she lived in one of the most expensive neighborhoods in the city." Nicholas raised his gaze to Aubrey's, facing her. "From what I understand, medical examiners earn quite a living. Were you assisting her financially so she could be closer to the school, or perhaps your parents helped pay her rent?"

"I… I wasn't helping her." Her gaze bounced between Nicholas, Dyson and Striker. Aubrey's bottom lip peeled from the top, the rise and fall of her shoulders slowing. She lowered both hands to her sides. "I don't know how she could afford to live here. When I asked, she'd laugh and change the subject."

"Is it possible she was seeing someone more well-off than she was or working a second job to supplement her income?" Striker asked. "Maybe she borrowed money from someone other than a bank?"

Color drained from the medical examiner's face as though she hadn't considered the possibility Kara could keep secrets from her. Seemed Aubrey and her sister weren't as close as the doc had believed. "No. Like I said, we talked every afternoon after she came home from work, even if I was at the hospital. No exceptions. She would've told me if she was in trouble. She would've known she could ask me for help."

"Dr. Flood, your sister was murdered sometime between 10:00 p.m. and 11:00 p.m. last night by a man, presumably in his late thirties, early forties, Caucasian, with extreme control, a hell of a lot of patience and an obsession with past serial cases." His gut twisted as she blanched, and Nicholas wished like hell there was a way to soften that blow. He closed the distance between them, his footsteps heavy as she straightened to confront his approach head-on. "This wasn't a random attack. Something about Kara appealed to her killer, and I have reason to believe she isn't the only one he has his sights set on."

"The way he replicated the X Marks the Spot Killer's MO suggests the killer has intimate knowledge of the case and possibly something to prove to Cole Presley," Dyson said.

The kid was right. "You worked that case, Aubrey. You were able to fill in the blanks when we had no other evidence or leads to follow. Without you, we would still be looking for him. What better way to get your attention than by targeting someone you care about?"

One breath. Two.

Aubrey shifted her weight between both feet then folded her arms across her chest. A defense tactic that had little power to ward off the truth. They weren't looking for a one-off killer here. She had to know that. She had to see the similarities between her sister's death and the X Marks the Spot case. "You both think whoever killed my sister is punishing me because I was able to identify Cole Presley. A family member for a family member."

"You told Agent James you believed that's why Kara was killed. We're here to find out if that's the case." Striker surveyed the apartment for herself, taking in every detail. "Dr. Flood, I specialize in missing persons cases, but some of the same profile points apply during a homicide investigation. Did Kara mention anything suspicious over the past few days? Someone who was paying more attention to her than usual? Was she visiting places she didn't normally go or receiving any threats?"

"She didn't mention anything like that." Aubrey's face smoothed, and Nicholas read the change in her demeanor for what it was. Denial. "But she told me Koko started barking in the middle of the night last week."

His instincts shot into awareness. "That's unusual?"

"Kara hired a professional trainer a few years ago because Koko was barking at anyone he didn't know. It took him a full week to get used to seeing me when Kara went out of town the first year she had him." Aubrey cast her honey-warm gaze to the floor, almost seeming to curl in on herself, and Nicholas drowned the urge to reach out. Emotions couldn't get involved in a case like this. Not if they were going to find the bastard who'd murdered an innocent woman last night. "She said he hadn't freaked out like that for months, like he was scared out of his mind. When she got out of bed to see what was bothering him, she found him trying to escape his kennel. He was barking at the door. She thought maybe he'd heard something in the hallway."

"Kidnappers and killers like to stalk their

prey, learn their habits and routines. They like to collect trophies, too." Striker leveled her attention on him, and an understanding passed between them. "I'll call in a forensic unit to run through the scene. Until then, you should search the apartment to see if anything might be missing." She headed into the hallway, careful not to touch the doorknob on her way out, with Dyson on her heels.

"Seattle PD hasn't reported any sightings of Kara's dog hanging around the scene. Officers are still knocking on doors to see if somebody saw something last night, but there's a chance he hasn't gone far. Is there anywhere you can think of Koko might go if he felt threatened? A neighbor he might've warmed up to over the past few months?" It was a long shot, but one they couldn't ignore.

"You want to see if he might have any evidence of the attack on him." She swiped her hand beneath her nose then pushed thick, dark brown hair out of her face. Another defense tactic meant to distract herself from the brutal images the doc would never be able to forget, he was sure. She extracted her phone. "Yeah, there's someone in the building who walks him when Kara's working. They have my phone number in case they can't reach Kara. I'll send you the information."

He gave her his number, and his phone pinged a moment later.

"Whoever did this—whoever killed Kara last night—it's a copycat, right?" Desperation combined with exhaustion in her expression, and his gut clenched. "Tell me we put the right man behind bars when you arrested Cole Presley, that I didn't make a mistake."

Heat burned down the length of his spine. The medical examiner was one of the most intelligent, compassionate, emotionally aware people he'd ever met, and he'd hate the day when her drive to find justice for the deceased ebbed. "You didn't make a mistake, Aubrey. I did."

"WHAT IN THE sweet potato fries do you mean?" This case had just started. How had Agent James already made a mistake? Aubrey battled against the pressure seemingly closing in from every wall of her sister's apartment and tried to take a full breath.

She shouldn't have come up here. She should've handed off the key to Kara's apartment and stayed downstairs like the good witness she was supposed to be. But some internal drive she didn't understand had urged her to insert herself in the case, to find out who'd done this to her family. Every book on those shelves stared out at her as though she were an impostor, someone who didn't belong here. She'd always watched out for Kara. Now it seemed as though her sister's apartment was accusing her of not being there when she'd needed Aubrey the most. Why Kara? If the killer was out to punish Aubrey for her role in the X Marks the Spot Killer case, why had he gone after Kara?

"What'd you say?" Confusion deepened the lines between the agent's dark blond eyebrows.

"What do you mean, you made a mistake?" Stress had an array of physical, emotional and mental effects on the body, but odd cartoon sayings had always had the ability to alleviate her stress levels. She shook her head and folded her arms across her chest. But no matter how many different sayings ran through her head right then, none of them would help soothe the grief bubbling under her skin. Muscle tension strained the joints at her elbows and shoulders. She'd found her sister dead this morning, had been within fifty feet of the killer when he'd taped the map to her door. "The King County Medical Examiner's Office hasn't even performed my sister's autopsy. There haven't been any chances for you to make a mistake on this case."

The muscles in his jaw ticked under the pressure of his back teeth. He stared at her as though trying to read her mind—profile her—but she'd developed an equal detachment from the deceased as he had with the living over the years. Nicholas James had been the case lead when they'd worked together three years ago. Despite his secretive, isolated demeanor, there was a vulnerability in his eyes, a need to prove himself. He'd spent his life studying the most minute psychological details that made up a person where she'd spent her career uncovering what made a person physically. They'd chosen different career paths, but in the end, they weren't so different. They both wanted to find whoever had strangled Kara. "I knew Cole Presley personally."

Aubrey stepped back. She couldn't think, couldn't breathe. "I… I don't understand."

"My father left our family when I was five. Cole Presley was there for us when we needed him. He helped me with my homework after school. He babysat me and my sister when my mom needed to go back to school. He taught me how to throw a damn baseball and coached my Little League team." Disbelief wove through each word, his voice getting heavier and heavier. "I had no idea who he really was. Not until you described the kind of blade that'd been used on the X Marks the Spot victims. You'd found slivers of western hemlock in one of the women's wounds. What you'd described—Damascus steel with a nick about a quarter inch down the blade and an intricate design pressed into the metal—

I could see it right in front of me. Because I'd seen that knife before. He used it to carve figurines from chunks of wood whenever we'd go camping together. I'd held it over a dozen times in my own hands without knowing how much blood had collected in the handle over the years."

Thirty years, to be exact. Thirty victims, every year on the same day.

Air caught in her throat. She wasn't sure what to say, what to do. Swiping her tongue over her increasingly dry lips, Aubrey countered her retreat, her feet heavier than when she'd watched him search Kara's apartment. Her pulse rocketed into her throat. A hint of soap and salt dived into her lungs. "When you said you made a mistake, you mean because you didn't see him for what he really was before. You feel personally responsible for what happened to all those women."

"Aren't I?" he asked. "The X Marks the Spot case was what inspired me to join the FBI, you know. I'd see the yearly newspaper article detailing how he'd strangled and mutilated another woman, how police were baffled he kept getting away with it."

She flinched at the manner in which he addressed the killer's MO—so insensitively—and severed eye contact as fast as she could.

"I'd tell myself I'd be the one to catch him someday. Come to find out, the killer was less than thirty feet from my own family." A humorless laugh burst from his mouth. "Guess I got my wish in the end. Maybe if I'd seen him for what he really was, so many people wouldn't have died. But I..."

"You trusted him." The same unsteady guilt in his voice clawed up her throat. She reached out, gripping his arm in a comforting squeeze despite the fact he'd bowled over the way her sister had died without a hint of regret. Then again, she'd always put others' needs first without acknowledging her own. Instant heat shot up through her hand, and she fought to chase back the weight crushing her from inside. "You gave me credit for bringing the X Marks the Spot Killer down, but the truth is, if it wasn't for you, Cole Presley would still be out there, hurting women. You recognized the blade he used to cut Xs into his victims' cheeks. That's why I requested you to work my sister's case. You're one of the most focused, insightful and realistic investigators I've ever worked with, and I need you to find out who did this to her."

"I'll find your sister's killer, Aubrey. I give you my word." Sincerity laced his voice, and a shiver chased down her spine. "But what do sweet potato fries have to do with anything?"

Heat climbed up her neck, and she withdrew her hand. She pressed her palm against her throat in an attempt to stop the embarrassment from taking over her face, but it was a battle she'd never won in the past. "I tend to repeat odd Southern sayings, mostly food or animal related, from a popular children's cartoon character when I'm under stress."

"A children's cartoon character?" Agent James stepped back, turning his focus to the wall of bookshelves. Historical romances, nonfiction educational resources, science fiction. Her sister never had been one to conform to the traditional sense of a kindergarten teacher. "I wasn't aware you had kids."

Was that shock in his expression? Satisfaction exploded from behind her sternum. Considering he'd had more than enough time to profile her from head to toe and inside out, she hadn't been sure it was possible to surprise him, and she stood a little taller. "I don't, but considering what I do for a living, I'd rather not indulge in crime dramas, hospital comedies or true crime documentaries. I'm sure it's the same for you with cop shows and profiling entertainment."

"You're right." A hint of a smile tugged at the corner of his mouth.

Her fingers tingled as she studied Kara's apartment a second time, and a hollowness set up residence in her chest. She curled her keys into her palm and forced the edge of steel deeper.

The oversensitive skin along the back of her neck heated. Agent James—Nicholas—had promised to find her sister's killer, but how many more family members would have to stand in the middle of their loved one's home to try to give the BAU a lead to follow? How many more victims would have to cross Dr. Caldwell's slab before this new evolution of killer was found? No. She wasn't going to let that happen. "It doesn't seem real. Kara not being here." Denial burned through her. She cleared her throat in an effort to bring herself back to the present and away from the growing familiarity between them. "I haven't noticed anything missing so far. Everything looks just like it did the last time I visited. Do you need to look at anything else while you're here?"

"No, I think we've got everything we need." He craned his chin over his shoulder, giving her a glimpse of the thick tendons running the length of his neck, as he took in one last study of the space.

"Good." Straightening, she gave in to the spread of confidence and headed toward the door. "Then we should check with Kara's dog walker to see if Koko has shown up."

His footsteps echoed off the laminate a split second before a strong hand threaded through the space between her rib cage and arm and twisted her into a solid wall of muscle. The color of his eyes deepened—physically impossible but evident in the intensity in which he stared down at her all the same. "I know it can't be easy for you to be here, Aubrey, especially given what you've already been through today, but I need you to let the BAU do their jobs without getting involved."

"I've spent my entire life bowing down to the needs of others, Agent James. I've dedicated my entire life to giving family members answers they needed as to how their loved ones passed. I've taken care of my parents physically and financially for years, even when I had nothing left to give. I've made the Seattle police, the FBI and, yes, even your unit my priority since I took over as chief medical examiner and have lost friendships and relationships in the process, but today, your needs don't concern me."

She tugged her arm from his grasp. Her elbow burned from the friction emanating from his touch, and she notched her chin higher, more defiant than she'd ever felt before. Her scalp tightened as she pressed her hand against his chest for room to breathe. Running her thumb over the notches in her sister's key, Aubrey stepped back. The rush of her pulse behind her ears died as logic returned. "Dr. Caldwell is a fine physician, but he's not me. He doesn't have serial experience, and you won't find another ME within four hundred miles who does. You want to find out who did this to my sister and keep more women from becoming victims? You're not going to be able to do that without me."

Nicholas steadied his gaze on hers. She could practically see the wheels spinning in his head as he considered the chances he had without her. His strong exhale deflated his shoulders as he stalked past her toward the door. "Then we're going to need some coffee."

Chapter Three

Talking with the victim's dog walker had ended in a dead end. The neighbor hadn't seen the white shepherd or heard anything unusual leading up to Kara Flood's death. Uniformed officers had cleared the rest of the building. No sign of the dog or statements anyone had seen the victim last night.

"We've got a handful of possible evidence walking around the city, and no one saw a damn thing." Nicholas shoved his notepad into his back pocket harder than necessary, but he had enough self-awareness and experience to know the missing dog was only a part of the equation that could lead them to the killer.

Apart from the unit discovering his childhood connection to the X Marks the Spot Killer during the investigation and being forced to see the bureau shrink after the arrest, he'd never told anyone about Cole Presley. Yet he'd willingly offered the information to Dr. Aubrey Flood. He hadn't considered himself manipulatable. In his line of work, that kind of influence could get him or any one of his teammates killed, but apparently, brilliant honey-warm eyes, an IQ notches beyond his and a mouth to die for was all he'd needed to spill his guts.

Both Nicholas and Aubrey pushed through the glass lobby doors of the apartment building and stepped into a thick coating of humidity. "Can you think of anywhere else the dog might go?"

Sorrow smoothed Aubrey's features as her attention flickered toward the bench where she'd found her sister's body this morning. She cleared her throat as though to bring herself back into the moment, but there was only so much she could do to distract herself before the pain caught up. As much as she'd claimed she needed to find Kara Flood's killer upstairs, there would always be a part of her battling to deny her younger sister had been murdered in the first place. That was how the human brain worked. It could only take so much trauma and confrontation before it would snap.

Aubrey recentered her anguished expression on him, and an internal sucker punch to the gut threatened to knock him off his feet. "He's been to my house a few times, but I wouldn't think it'd be somewhere he'd automatically go if he was in distress."

She'd lost her sister, one of the most important people in her world. While Nicholas couldn't do anything to undo that kind of violence, he'd sure as hell find the son of a bitch to keep her from looking at him like that ever again. "Better safe than sorry." He unclipped the radio from his belt and pinched the push-to-talk button between his thumb and index finger. "Striker, come in."

The radio crackled. "Go ahead."

"CSU is wrapping up down here at the scene, and no one has seen the dog. Where is my other team?" He surveyed the crowd of onlookers beyond the perimeter of the tape, memorizing their faces. Killers had a habit of returning to the scenes of their crimes, especially budding serials who may have just stepped into the violent crimes arena. The serials he'd investigated liked to see the damage caused, revel in the family's grief, relive the events that led to the life draining from their victim's eyes at their hand. But worse, some used the opportunity of being able to blend into a crowd to choose a new victim. Revisiting the scene kept them going just as solving the case kept Nicholas going. Any one of these onlookers could be the killer they were looking for.

"The second unit is twenty minutes out," Striker said. "You want me to wait for them?"

A flash registered from beyond the tape and

pulled his attention to a single male, around six feet with dull red hair, a thick beard turning lighter around his temples. The man lowered a camera slowly, steady gaze aware Nicholas had spotted him.

"James, you copy?" Striker asked.

Aubrey followed his gaze toward the man who'd taken the photo.

He lifted the radio back to his mouth. "Dyson can wait for them. I need you and West to help Seattle PD wrap up the scene and oversee getting the evidence they've collected so far to the lab," he said. "I'm going to accompany Dr. Flood to her residence to search there in case Fido is waiting for her to come home and grab a few overnight items before relocating her to the safe house."

"His name is Koko, Agent James," Aubrey said. "Not Fido."

He released the push-to-talk button. Studying the man beyond the perimeter tape, he brushed off the awareness of the medical examiner's gaze, determined to burn a hole through his temple. An immediate detachment from the vulnerability she'd resurrected in him took control.

"Confirmed," Striker said. "I'm still waiting to hear back from the warden at Washington State Corrections on Presley's location. I'll keep you apprised of any developments. Striker, out."

"You're taking me to a safe house." Aubrey shook her head. Anger intertwined with the fire burning in her eyes. Medium-length brown hair lifted off her shoulders and caught on her eyelashes. Pointing a finger into his chest, she stepped into him, her voice low. "You had no intention of letting me work this case with you, did you? As long as I'm in a safe house with some other agent from your unit, you'll be free to investigate my sister's case on your own, but I can promise you right now, that's not how this is going to work."

He met her intimidation technique with one of his own, closing the distance between them until her exhales brushed against his neck. "The killer knows who you are, Dr. Flood. He knows where you live, where you work, how many hours you spend in the hospital, whom you care about, your running route and your favorite places to eat. He knew exactly when you'd be home to leave that map on your door, and he knows you were the medical examiner assigned to the X Marks the Spot case three years ago. He's done his research, just as I've done mine, and if you have any chance of surviving what comes next, it will be because of me." Nicholas clipped the radio to his belt and extended an arm toward the perimeter tape and his SUV on the other side. "The way I see it, you have two choices. Agree to federal protection and help me find the man who killed your sister, or continue denying you're in danger and take your chances alone."

She didn't move, didn't even seem to breathe, and admiration knotted in his gut. Most suspects hadn't been able to handle the intensity he radiated during interrogations, and Dr. Flood—Aubrey—had given every single one of them a run for their money by facing off with him. She peeled away and headed straight from the scene toward his vehicle.

A smile tugged at the corners of his mouth as he followed her. Damn, she was something else. Warmhearted and friendly dosed with a strong helping of defiance and drive. Hell of a combination. Nicholas hauled the crime scene tape over his head and maneuvered through the civilians who'd parted to let her pass.

A strong grip latched on to his arm, and it took everything inside him not to reach for his weapon. He spun to face the man who'd grabbed him and wrenched away from the six-foot, red-headed photographer he'd noted earlier. Nervousness radiated from the man in waves, his hands shaking around his camera as he spoke. "You're Agent James, right? With the FBI's Behavioral Analysis Unit? You must be here to investigate a violent homicide if they called your unit in. I remember you from the X Marks the Spot Killer case."

"You're familiar with that case?" Onlookers and civilians shifted around him, hoping to hear insight as to what'd happened in their very own neighborhood. "What's with the camera?"

"Oh, I'm training to be a crime scene photographer for the Seattle Police Department. Simon Curry." He lifted the camera slightly, an old-looking device that'd seen better days, before extending his hand. Curry withdrew as Nicholas merely stared down at the photographer's hand. "And I'm not just familiar with the X Killer's case, I'm familiar with you, too. I've been studying your career since you started with the BAU, Agent James. The work you've done here in Seattle with serials is changing the way the FBI investigates violent crime." Disbelief widened the man's small eyes, and he stumbled back a step. "If you're here, that must mean you believe this is a serial case."

Gasps echoed around him, followed by a rush of whispered murmurs and questions. This wasn't his area. Caitlyn Yang, the public relations liaison between Seattle PD and the BAU, handled what information to reveal to the public and the timeline when that information would be made public. He raised his voice over the mass but doubted anything he had to say would ease the panic buzzing around him.

"All right. We are at the beginning of this investigation. The FBI is not ready to conclude that the death that occurred in front of this building this morning is the result of a serial working in the area." He caught sight of Aubrey Flood through the crowd, her light gaze steady on his, and a calm washed over him. "Once we have more information, so will you, and that's all I'm willing to say on the matter."

He wound his way through a barrage of questions and shouts and headed across the street toward his SUV. Unlocking the door remotely, he rounded the front of the vehicle and wrenched open Aubrey's door for her. Once inside, he collapsed into his own seat behind the wheel. He twisted the key in the ignition, keeping her in his peripheral vision as he pulled away from the curb. "You okay?"

"I think they were more interested in you than they were me." Aubrey slid her palms down her thighs, staring out the passenger-side window. "I left my car parked in Kara's lot. It's probably going to get towed, since I don't have one of those HOA stickers. She offered to get me one, but..."

"It felt like lying." Her honest nature wouldn't have let her take advantage of her sister's offer.

"I'll have Agent West ensure it's secure and drive it back to your apartment as soon as he, Dyson and Agent Striker are finished at the scene. The farther you're away from your residence and vehicle, the better until we find out why Kara was targeted." An uneasy sensation surged through him, and he raised his gaze to the rearview mirror. A single figure stood in the center of the street as the mob of civilians dispersed along the scene's perimeter tape. Simon Curry lifted his camera toward his face, and a flash filled the mirror.

NOTHING AND EVERYTHING had changed since she'd found that map taped to her apartment door this morning. Her building looked exactly the same. Contrasting shades of gray highlighted six floors of lofts a mere two blocks from the heart of the city. But where she'd woken with enthusiasm and confidence for the day, hollowness had taken control. Kara was dead, and there hadn't been anything she'd been able to do about it.

The Space Needle demanded attention out Aubrey's passenger window as Nicholas pulled into her underground garage. She handed the agent her fob to the gate and sat back in her seat as the vehicle crawled forward into darkness. Kara hadn't just died. Her younger sister had become a homicide victim, something Aubrey dealt with day in and day out as the city's chief medical examiner, but this… This was different. This was personal. "The doorman should be able to tell us whether or not Koko came here when we get to the lobby."

"The building has a doorman?" Nicholas's eyes narrowed as he pulled the SUV into her assigned parking spot for her loft. His tone had leveled again. Nothing like the intensity he'd used in Kara's apartment. More inquisitive. He shoved the vehicle into Park. "Makes me wonder how the killer managed to get to your apartment."

The blood drained from her face and rushed directly to her chest, a flight-or-flight response automated by the body when faced with danger and fear. She hadn't thought of that. She wasn't an investigator in the way Nicholas was. She had experience with a serial killer's work through a single case, but it'd been years since she'd had to deal with emergency situations like this. Aubrey set her hand against the passenger-side door. He was right. She'd been so focused on what'd happened to Kara, her brain hadn't caught on to the fact the killer had walked straight into this building and directly to her door. He'd known where she lived, when she would be home. How? How had he known where to find her?

"You're looking a little pale there, Doc," Nicholas said.

"I'm dizzier than a donkey trying to dance." She focused on the way he called her "Doc," on the slight inflection in his voice when he spoke to her compared to his team or even those people at the perimeter of the scene. Her heart picked up the pace as he took a brick from the invisible professional barrier between them. *Doc*. No one had given her a nickname before. "I just need a minute."

"I've got to start writing down the stuff you say for future reference." Nicholas shouldered out of the vehicle. Faster than she thought possible, her door disappeared out from beneath her hand, and he was reaching over her for the seat belt. A combination of salt and man filled her lungs, and she breathed in as much as she could to hold on to his scent a bit longer. Strong enough to overpower the odor of decomposing bodies and formaldehyde. Soothing. Reassuring. "Come on. I've got you."

The seat belt released as he compressed the latch, and then his hands were on her. Strong, calloused—as though he reveled in manual labor in addition to catching psychopaths—comforting. She wound the straps of her purse around her hand. Butterflies twisted her stomach as Nicholas helped her from the SUV and closed the door behind her. Hand leveraged on the vehicle's frame above her head, he leaned into her while giving her the opportunity to slide out of his reach. "Most people never see a body in their lifetime. Sometimes it takes a while for the brain to process that kind of trauma."

"I feel like you should be aware of the fact we met during the X Marks the Spot Killer's victims' autopsies." The sarcasm earned her a smile that tightened her insides and brought the feeling back to her fingers. The world washed away into overhydrated watercolors under his focus.

"You're right. You're not most people." The curl of his mouth deepened the laugh lines etched from the middle of his nose and cut through the sharpness of his cheekbones. Thick eyebrows, matching his natural hair color, shadowed his gaze as he shifted his weight between his feet. He lowered his arm from above her head, and instantly, the spell was broken. Curling his hand into a fist, he tapped the side of the SUV as though punishing himself for letting her see the softer side of his personality. "That doesn't change the fact that the body you found this morning is someone you knew. Someone you loved. It's going to take time to work through the emotions that come with losing your sister like that, and you're going to need someone to help you through it."

She locked her back teeth against the urge to claim otherwise, to deflect her obsession with being everything for everyone but herself, to make it easier for the agent to remain comfortable and detached from her. But as easily as Nicholas James presented an intense, secretive and isolated mask to the world, he'd spoken from experience. He'd lost who she imagined to be one of the few people he'd let see the man hiding under that defensive mask. While Cole Presley— aka the X Marks the Spot Killer—hadn't been murdered as Kara had, and had in fact been the one to do the killing, Nicholas had lost that connection all the same. Aubrey broke eye contact, clearing her throat. "Coulter Loxley."

Nicholas took a step back, seemingly reminded of where they were and why. "Coulter Loxley?"

"The doorman. He would've been the one on shift last night when the killer came up to my apartment. We should talk to him, see if he remembers anything and ask if he's seen Koko." Aubrey clutched the straps of her bag tighter, the leather protesting under her grip. She checked her watch. "The only problem is he won't be on shift for another two hours."

Nicholas nodded. "In that case, I want to check your apartment to make sure there aren't any signs of a break-in and have you pack an overnight bag for a few days."

"Right." Because a killer had brought her into

his sick mind game by tacking a map leading to her sister's body to her door last night. Her throat tightened as she led the way toward the elevators and hit the ascend button. Seconds ticked by, maybe a minute when neither of them moved or said a word. What else was there to say? The elevator dinged before the car doors slid open, and they both stepped in. She scanned her key card that would give the elevator permission to stop at her floor, then leaned against the handrail surrounding them from three sides. Pressure to break the silence stretching between them, to make a connection with the man so familiar with murder, spread through her. Aubrey clutched her bag in front of her, the steel of the elevator doors reflecting her vain attempt to protect herself back at her. Diverting her nervous energy to the LED panel above the doors, she silently counted off the floors as they rocketed to the top floor. The penthouse.

"Does every resident have one of those cards?" he asked.

"No. Just the ones who live on the sixth floor." She studied the card, almost as though reading his mind. The killer would've had to have had one to gain access from the garage. "But visitors can access the floor from the stairs once they're past the doorman."

Silence descended once again.

"You said the X Marks the Spot Killer case is what inspired you to join the Behavioral Analysis Unit," she said. "How old were you when you decided you wanted to hunt killers for a living?"

His muscled shoulders rose on a strong inhale. He stared straight ahead, never deviating from his own reflection in front of him. "Six."

"Most kids that age want to grow up to be cowboys and astronauts or robots." The pull on her insides increased as the elevator dared to defy gravity. "There must've been a specific moment or event that made you feel profiling serial killers was the right path for you. Before you realized who your next-door neighbor was, I mean."

The tic of his external carotid artery just below his jaw increased. He dropped his chin a fraction of an inch and exposed her awareness of his every move. "I heard a woman scream."

A woman's scream? Regret cut through her as the implications of that single statement registered. Had he known who lived next door to him, even as young as six years old?

"I ran to the window to see what'd happened, but it was too dark. Every night afterward, for years, I'd wonder who it came from, why it occurred. I asked neighbors if they'd heard it that night. I started writing down their statements and seeing if my dog could pick up traces of blood around my house." He folded his hands in front of him. "Never found out what happened, but I knew then what I wanted to do with the rest of my life. I wanted to keep people from screaming like that ever again."

"Was it…" Aubrey licked her lips, trying to come up with another reason a woman might've been screaming in the middle of the night. "Do you believe it was one of Cole Presley's victims?"

The elevator dinged, pulling her back into reality as the car settled and the doors parted. Light fractured through massive windows and crawled across light gray hardwood flooring laid out in long strips designed to increase the visual size of the loft.

"I'll never know. I never found evidence he'd killed any of his victims in his home." Nicholas stepped off the elevator into her apartment and scanned the space like the good agent he was supposed to be. "It's unlikely the killer didn't know you'd need a key card to access this floor, which means he had to have come up the stairs to deliver the map he left on your door."

"The front door is around the corner." She motioned to her right as she stepped off the elevator and set her purse on the entryway table nearby. "The building's head of security should be able to give you any surveillance footage from last night if you ask nicely."

"I've already got Agent West working on it." Hands on his hips, he accentuated the shoulder holster and weapon under his jacket as he took in her living space. Nicholas turned toward the short hallway leading to the front door, and she followed. Unlocking the dead bolt, he compressed the door handle down and crouched to put the lock at his eye level. "It's just you here? No one else has a key? An ex-boyfriend, maybe?"

"Is that your way of asking me if I'm single, Agent James?" She kept her smile to herself, but tension crept across her back the longer he didn't answer. "No. There's no one else. I live alone."

He straightened, pointing toward the security ring on the outside of the door. "See these scratches here? Someone picked this lock recently, and I have good reason to believe it was your sister's killer."

SHE'D STOPPED BEING afraid of the monsters a long time ago.

Special Agent Madeline Striker couldn't look away from the little girl at the edge of the perimeter tape. Five or six years old, long, dark hair, brilliant, knowing eyes. The same age her sister had been the last time Madeline had seen her.

It wasn't because the monsters weren't real. The violence that'd led to the end of Kara Flood's life—and so many others during her five-year career with the Behavioral Analysis Unit—testified to that fact. They were out there, waiting for the right time to strike, working their mind games and preying on the innocent, but they couldn't control her. Not anymore.

She'd dedicated every day of her life to seeing how the pieces fit together, to connecting the dots in lost-cause abduction cases in an attempt to bring home as many victims as she could, but this case… They hadn't been prepared for this. It'd taken the entire BAU to identify and stop Cole Presley from taking another victim, but all they'd managed to do was create another monster. A copycat.

"Dr. Flood's vehicle is secure." Dashiell West slid into her peripheral vision. Dark, styled hair caught in the breeze coming off the sound. The five-o'clock shadow around his mouth and running up his jaw had grown thicker over the past few hours, highlighting the exhaustion under his eyes and in his voice. The tinkling of keys reached her ears as he tossed them her way. "You okay with following me to the ME's apartment to drop it off then giving me a lift back to the office?"

She caught the keys against her chest, forcing her gaze from the girl. To prove she could. A young woman matching the X Killer's preferences had been strangled and mutilated in front of her own apartment building eight hours ago, and no one had seen a damn thing. This wasn't an abduction case, but the clock was ticking down all the same. Copycats followed patterns, same as their role models. Whoever'd gotten to Kara Flood last night had already killed one victim. It was only a matter of time before he targeted another. "Yeah."

"Striker, you okay?" West leveled dark chocolate eyes on her. The former hotshot from the tech development arena had only been with the unit for two years after a former colleague had set out to ruin his career, but he'd been a vital addition to the team ever since. Cybercrimes, decryption, hacking—if a BAU case involved computers, it involved Dashiell West.

Reality caught up. Madeline glanced in the direction where she'd last seen the girl, finding the section of tape where she'd been standing empty. She swept the scene, but the girl had most likely been whisked back to the safety of her home with parents who'd do anything to keep her close. Gripping her hand around the keys her partner had thrown, she shook her head as though the past would dissolve at her command. "I'm fine. Have there been any developments on the Seattle PD side?"

Faint barking broke through the ringing in her ears.

"Last I heard, their crime scene unit was taking a casting of a footprint they found in the soil around one of the trees lining the street," he said. "Could be our guy, but considering how careful the killer was to not be seen by witnesses and how there isn't much evidence to collect, the chances are low."

The barking continued. Madeline turned toward the sound. Nicholas had asked her to keep a watch for a white shepherd the victim had been walking at the time of her death, but the dog hadn't turned up in the building or in the area. No leash. No paw prints, blood or anything else that would give her an idea of where the dog might have run after the attack. Nothing. Except the barking. "Do you hear that?"

"What?" West asked.

"That barking." She headed toward the south side of the scene, and the sound intensified. Hauling the perimeter tape above her head, she moved slowly down the street, West close behind. Sweat pooled in her shirt. Summer in Seattle promised cooler temperatures considering the proximity of the Pacific but had really only delivered humidity that frizzed her hair and drenched her clothing.

The barking stopped, and Madeline froze.

Nails scratched on metal from somewhere nearby, and she spotted a white cargo van parked along the street ahead. If Kara Flood's dog had gotten back into the habit of protesting any time a stranger came near as Dr. Flood had said, it was possible the killer would want the dog out of the way before attracting attention during the attack. She nodded toward the van and unholstered her weapon. "West."

West understood, withdrawing his own side-arm, and stepped out into the street to approach from the other side of the van.

Nicholas had taught her some killers liked to revisit their crime scenes, that they enjoyed the hunt brought on by law enforcement, reveled in watching the police try to do their jobs and staying one step ahead. Madeline checked back over her shoulder, gauging how far she and West had walked from the crime scene. From the angle of the driver's seat, whoever sat behind the wheel would have the perfect vantage point of the bench where Kara Flood had been posed.

They moved as one, West on one side of the van, her on the other, until they met at the bumper. Her partner reached for the swinging door's handle, those dark eyes on her as he waited for her signal. The front seats were clear, but without windows in the cargo area, they had no way to tell what was on the other side of the doors. Madeline nodded, and West wrenched the door open.

Ear-shattering barking echoed off the inside of the cabin a split second before a white shepherd, matching Dr. Flood's description of her sister's dog, came into view. Spots of dirt stained the dog's once-pristine coat. Madeline holstered her weapon and showed Koko both hands, palms forward. "Hey, Koko. It's okay. I'm not here to hurt you." She turned toward West. "Let Nicholas know we found his missing piece of evidence and call Animal Control to take him in. Not Nicholas, the dog."

The canine whined, sitting back on its haunches, and revealed a numbered piece of paper under his paws. Something like the numbers she'd seen on the back side of photos. She pulled a set of gloves from her pocket and snapped the latex against the back of her wrist. One hand raised toward Koko, she collected the glossy paper from under the dog's foot slower than she wanted to go. No point in scaring the poor animal. He'd already been through enough.

He let the photo go, and Madeline pulled herself out of the van. Flipping the evidence over with one hand, she gasped as West brought his phone to his ear, her heart in her throat. She turned the picture toward him. "Then tell him we've got another victim out there."

Chapter Four

The killer had broken into Aubrey's home, most likely touched her personal effects and uncovered details she hadn't wished to share with anyone else. Rage coiled low in his gut as the forensic team he'd pulled in swept the loft for fingerprints and anything that could give them an idea of who'd gotten inside.

Floor-to-ceiling windows looked out toward surrounding redbrick buildings. Light furniture, hardly used as far as Nicholas could tell, and pops of color in accents brightened the space. Black-and-white modern art pieces had been paired in twos on almost every wall with a beautiful kitchen island and patio that finished off the luxury feel. The aesthetic could've come straight out of a home decor magazine, but it wasn't exactly reflective of the kind of home he'd expected from the medical examiner. Too…cold. Distant. Definitely not the haven Kara Flood escaped to every night after work.

Crime scene techs worked their way across the loft, including the bookcases on either side of a large television screen. In an instant, he imagined Aubrey curled up on the L-shaped fabric sectional watching her favorite children's show to unwind after a long day of autopsies, facing grieving families and pathology reports. Not in her bedroom packing a few days' worth of clothing and toiletries to hide in a safe house from a violent killer.

He scanned the titles stacked in neat color-coded rows on her bookshelves and pulled one from the pack. A romance. Flipping through the pages, he studied the pliancy of the spine. Not just a romance. A book worthy of multiple reads. A favorite. Nicholas placed it back on the shelf and continued down the line. More romance, some inspirational nonfiction. Where her sister had been firmly rooted in reality as an educator, Aubrey obviously craved escape from her day-to-day routine, and he sure as hell didn't blame her.

"There's a perfume bottle missing from my bathroom. I've given your people permission to search through whatever they need, but that looks like the only thing that might've been taken." Aubrey maneuvered into his peripheral vision with a crime scene tech delivering her back to the living room. They couldn't take any chances of altering or destroying evidence of the break-in. Not when the killer had obviously set his sights on the ME. She clutched the handle of her carry-on–size luggage. Her gaze then lowered to a book still in his hand. "Didn't peg you for a romance reader."

Perfume bottle. A possible trophy? But how had the killer gotten past the building's security measures? He set the novel back on the shelf and pushed the book between the others with one finger. "Guaranteed happily-ever-after, no matter how wrong things go? Beats reality any day. What's not to like?"

"I agree." A small smile turned up the corners of her mouth as he'd revealed yet another piece of himself without hesitation, and his insides coiled tighter. "The doorman should be coming on to shift right about now. The elevator bypasses the lobby and goes straight to the parking garage, so it's better to take the stairs."

"CSU is almost finished here. I'll make sure they lock up when they're done." He motioned her toward the front door and stepped into line behind her. His phone vibrated with an incoming call, and he pulled it from his slacks without missing a step. Dashiell West. Hitting the large green button at the bottom of the screen, he brought his phone to his ear as they left the apartment. "What's going on, West?"

"We found the dog," West said.

Nicholas slid his hand around Aubrey's arm and turned her into him. He lowered the phone between them and put the call on speakerphone. "You're sure you've got the right dog?"

"White shepherd, approximately three years old with a collar that says his name is Koko. We're double-checking the chip in his neck, but Striker and I are ninety-nine percent sure this is the victim's dog. Whoever killed Kara Flood last night had locked the animal in a cargo van less than a block from the scene. Damn cabin got to over a hundred degrees by the time we found him. If it weren't for Striker's superhero hearing, we might never have found him in time." Admiration tinted the former tech expert's voice. "The dog was dehydrated and a bit disoriented, but Animal Services is taking care of that right now. I've got Forensics collecting particulates from his fur, but it sounds like he's going to be fine."

Nicholas raised his gaze to Aubrey's in time to see pure relief slacken her expression. "Thanks, West. I'll get in touch with Forensics when they're finished. You did good."

"That's not all we recovered from the van," West said. "After we were able to calm the dog down, we realized he'd been standing on a photo. A Polaroid."

Confusion quickly replaced the excitement buzzing in his veins. Nicholas switched the phone off speaker and raised it to his ear. He'd wanted Aubrey to know her sister's dog had been located safely from the source who'd recovered the animal, but the last thing she needed to hear were the gory details of Kara's case. "A Polaroid of what?"

"A body. A woman." Silence settled between them as dread pooled at the base of Nicholas's spine. Another victim. "We don't have an ID yet, but I'm running facial recognition as we speak. Nicholas, the woman… There's no doubting the photo was taken after she'd been killed. Whoever murdered Kara Flood last night used the X Marks the Spot Killer's MO. Strangulation, mutilation to the victim's face with a thin blade. He locked up the victim's dog in a cargo van reported stolen in the last three days and left a photo of his next victim for us to find."

A trail of bread crumbs for law enforcement to follow. Nausea churned in his gut as the next piece of the puzzle fit into place. A photo left with a victim's body, leading police to the next. Just as the Gingerbread Woman had done. He turned away from Aubrey and lowered his voice. "Are the woman's lips blue in the photo?"

"Yes, with her jacket positioned beside her," West said. "I've already sent a copy to Dr. Caldwell at the King County Medical Examiner's Office since he's taken lead on Kara Flood's autopsy. He's positive the woman in the photo died of asphyxiation within two hours of the picture being taken."

Damn it. Running his hand through his hair, he processed the details of the Gingerbread Woman case. There hadn't been anything linking Irene Lawrence—the woman who'd suffocated five rival colleagues for a shot at partner within her law firm—to the X Marks the Spot Killer. The cases weren't connected, but whoever killed Kara Flood last night wanted him to believe they were, that there was more than one killer they were hunting. He shook his head. No. His instincts said one killer, two MOs. "The killer is testing previously used MOs, trying to find the one that's right for him. He wanted us to find Kara Flood first. He used the X Marks the Spot Killer's MO because that's whom he looks up to the most, probably because of how long it took law enforcement to identify Cole Presley. He sees a thirty-year reign as a sign of success. Now he's moving on to another MO."

"The Gingerbread Woman." West swore under his breath. "Is there any way to tell whose MO he'll use next or something that will help us narrow down the identity of this victim?"

"This killer locked the dog up because he needed Koko to ensure we recovered that photo. He's not fueled by anger. He's not out to make these women pay. He wants an audience like the good narcissist he is." Nicholas set his forehead against the nearest wall and let himself slip into the mind of the killer, pushing two separate cases together in an attempt to find common ground. It wasn't his soundproof office he'd turned into a dark room back at BAU headquarters, but he'd done this exercise enough times over the years to drop into the meditation-like frequency to separate himself from the world. There was a risk to doing it here. If he pulled out too quickly, he'd spend the rest of the day paying the price. Why had the killer chosen those two MOs to kill his victims? If he could solve that variable, he might be able to predict which MO the killer would use next and narrow down a possible victim.

The chaotic organization of the forensics team burrowed into his head, and he mentally pulled out before he had a chance to dive deep enough. Damn it. He needed somewhere quiet. Somewhere he could control the setting. His heart thundered hard behind his ears. Different MOs meant there was no pattern for them to follow. The killer didn't have a preference in regard to the victim or a motive to want them dead. Whoever had killed Kara Flood and this possible second victim simply believed he could do his heroes' work better. "I'm going to have to call you back."

Nicholas ended the call, all too aware of Aubrey standing behind him.

"Are you all right?" Her voice, more sincere than he wanted it to be, slid through him and battled to soothe the haunted memories he carried from his previous cases. She maneuvered into his peripheral vision, concern and compassion clear in the way she tentatively reached toward him but never made contact. "I'll get you some water." She retraced her steps toward her apartment door, her luggage still in hand.

He curled one hand under her arm to stop her from leaving, and the buzz in his head died in an instant. His heart rate dropped. His breathing evened out. "I'm fine. It's…" Nicholas pried his hand from her arm, and the buzz in his head returned. Her hypnotic honey-colored gaze settled on him, encouraging him to explain. "I have a unique way of profiling killers. It's kind of like dropping into a meditation. Nothing exists for me outside what I see in my head, and I get disoriented if I pull out too quickly."

"Like when divers surface from deep water too quickly, they get the bends." Not a question, and a completely accurate comparison. Aubrey stepped toward him, raising her hands to his face. "You're able to disassociate yourself from everyone and everything around you. I've read psychological journals detailing the theory. Deep meditation has many benefits for the brain and physical body. May I?"

He nodded, not really sure what she was asking his permission for until she set her fingers around his neck. She tested his pulse at the base of his throat, and the warmth of her skin anchored him to the moment.

"Headaches, dizziness, disorientation, ringing in your ears, that kind of thing?" Aubrey raised her index finger a few inches from his nose, and he followed it back and forth. "Are you experiencing any of them now?"

Amazement spread through him as he ran a mental check through his entire body. He was beginning to see why the killer had come here, to take something of hers in an effort to get close. "Not in the least."

THERE WAS ANOTHER victim out there.

She'd overheard Nicholas's call with Agent West. A photo of a woman had been recovered after the BAU had located Koko in the back of a cargo van mere feet from the perimeter of the scene where she'd found Kara.

"We'll be at the safe house in a few minutes," Nicholas said. "You'll be able to rest, get something to eat, clean up."

"I don't need to rest. I need to find who killed my sister." Questioning the doorman of her building hadn't resulted in any new leads. Coulter Loxley specifically remembered an ambulance pulling up to the doors in response to a 9-1-1 call on the floor below hers around the time Nicholas had narrowed down the killer's entry into her building. He'd let the emergency responders inside without hesitation, leaving whoever'd taped the map to her door to use the distraction to his advantage. Only afterward had the EMTs informed him the call had been a hoax. No one on the floor below had needed emergency attention. At least, not that they'd been able to confirm. And the footage from the cameras positioned around the lobby between 10:00 p.m. and 11:00 p.m. last night had been compromised despite security's insistence that was impossible.

Aubrey curled her fingers into her palms, traces of his body heat still absorbed into her hands as they drove away from her loft through the blurred streets of the city. She hadn't been a practicing physician for three years, but helping those in need had been the reason she'd gone to medical school to study pathology in the first place. Nicholas had needed her help. Disorientation, slightly slurred speech. She stared down at her fingers and forced herself to release her grip. Crescent-moon indents lingered near the base of her palms.

A few seconds. That was all it'd taken to exterminate the cold deep that'd settled behind her sternum when she'd measured his pulse under her bare fingers. It'd been erratic and thready, as though he'd woken from a nightmare, his skin slightly filmed with sweat, yet he'd been conscious. Highly insightful, perceptive, even cerebral, Nicholas James wasn't like any other FBI agent she'd worked with in her tenure as Seattle's chief medical examiner. The muscles along her throat constricted, and she blinked back the involuntarily emotion burning in her eyes. If it weren't for Kara, she never would've made the career change from research into clinical practice. Ironic now that Aubrey would use that hands-on knowledge to find her sister's killer. "I used to make my sister pretend to be a corpse when we were little."

The weight of Nicholas's full attention landed on her, and her heart rate ticked up a few notches. "Is that one of those weird sayings you spout when you're in a stressful situation, or did you actually make your sister pretend to be a corpse?"

"Kara would stage her death all over the house, and it was my job to figure out how she'd died. It was a game we played. We called it Murder-Suicide. I was very good at discovering cause of death. It's one of the reasons why I became a medical examiner." A humorless smile tugged at the corners of her mouth as the memories washed over her. "One morning, I woke up and found her asleep with her head in the oven in an apparent suicide, but I proved it was murder."

Nicholas cringed, sinking lower in his seat with one hand still on the wheel. "What the hell kind of house did you grow up in?"

"My parents encouraged us to explore all kinds of knowledge. My father was a science teacher at the local high school, and my mother was an anthropologist." Her pride echoed in her own ears. "They ensured we followed a career path that would make us happy."

"And cutting up dead people makes you happy?" he asked.

The convulsion in her gut hit as though he'd physically attacked her. "Being a pathologist isn't solely about cutting up dead people, Agent James. It's about learning how disease works inside the human body so vaccinations can be made. It's about giving loved ones answers as to why their family member passed away in his sleep. It's about helping bring a murderer to justice by studying how he attacked his victim, how much force he used and whether or not it was a crime of passion or premeditated."

Her sister's words. Not many people understood her career choice—friends, extended family, the men she'd dated over the years—but Kara had. Up until the past few years, when they'd gotten into a habit of talking of nothing but their parents. No matter how hard Aubrey had tried, she and Kara couldn't seem to connect as they had when they were children. Of all the people who should see the connection they had in common, she thought it would've been Nicholas. She took the bite out of her voice and stared out the window as loss charged up her throat. The roller coaster of grief would be a never-ending ride of pain—for years—and there wasn't a damn thing she could do about it. "Kara was the one who convinced me to leave research and publishing to pursue more clinical work. She said if anyone could give the dead a voice, it would be me."

"We're going to find whoever did this to your sister, Aubrey." He maneuvered the SUV off the main street onto a paved one-way road that ran along the length of a few warehouses. "But you're right. I'm sorry. What I said was insensitive."

Salmon Bay glittered out beyond the windshield, rows of boats and waterfront condos bright against the reflection of the sky off the water. She hadn't realized how long they'd been driving north, lost in her own head as the case grew even more complicated. "To be honest, it isn't much worse than what I've heard from the men I've dated and my friends. People who aren't in the medical field or law enforcement don't really understand what I do. They see it more as morbid fascination than anything. It's hard for them to relate, so I tend to alienate conversation when I talk about my job. My career choice and my dedication to my work has ended more relationships than I care to admit."

"Sounds like you need new friends. As for the men you've dated, anybody who doesn't see you for the generous and understanding woman you are is an idiot." The SUV's shocks absorbed the speed bumps leading down to the waterfront, and Nicholas turned onto another side road, bringing them parallel to the bay before slowing. Parking, he studied the wide expanse of docks, boats and trees in front of them. "Here we are. It's not much, but it's more than enough to keep anyone from finding you for a few days."

Aubrey shouldered out of the car and dropped into pressed, tire-casted dirt. The wind blew her hair back behind her shoulders and kicked up the scents of salt, mud and algae. The industrial chic shipping container–turned–condo had been outfitted with oversize windows, sliding glass doors and a bright turquoise paint color that stood out among the rest of those on the same row. Lapping water reached her ears, and doubt curdled in her stomach. "This is a shipping container. The FBI uses this as a safe house?"

"Wait until you see the inside." Nicholas

closed his door behind him and gathered their
bags from the back seat with a wink in her direction. He hauled his duffel bag over his shoulder—something he must keep in his vehicle for
any situation—and dragged her suitcase behind
him. "Shipping containers are the new double-
wide trailers, and if we get into some trouble, all
they have to do is load us on a boat instead of a
truck." His laugh fed confidence into her veins,
and she realized he'd made a joke. "Come on,
Doc. You've got nothing to worry about."

She studied the configuration of three containers, two on the bottom, one stacked on top, and
followed him around to the east entrance. The
punch of a keypad reached her ears before Nicholas pushed inside, a glint in his green-blue eyes.

Light gray wall paint with white trim registered as she stepped over the threshold. Equally
light hardwood flooring ran the length of the two
containers that'd been welded together to create
a warm and unexpectedly inviting atmosphere.
The kitchen off to her right with gray cabinets
and a wood block countertop didn't compare to
the one back at her loft, but it promised to do exactly as Nicholas had suggested. Not much but
more than enough. A small breakfast bar with
two stools met her a few feet into the home, with
a hallway on the other side leading to a dining
room and living space at the back. A set of stairs

branched off to her left, which she assumed led to the bedrooms on the second level and most likely a bathroom.

Nicholas studied her with too much intensity—she couldn't hold his gaze. He wheeled her suitcase in front of her, handing it off. "As you can see, it's not hard to get the lay of the land. The bedrooms are up those stairs, and I use that term loosely. There are two queen-size beds on opposite sides of the house without doors. Feel free to take whichever your heart desires."

No doors. Just opposite sides of the shipping container he'd brought her to. Eighteen hours ago, her life had been as normal and routine as it could get. It hadn't been reduced to hiding from a narcissistic killer who'd murdered her sister and started a mind game she couldn't understand.

She pressed the bar of her suitcase into the lock position. Someone had broken into her home, had gone through her things, studied her. She wanted to go back to her loft, to her routine, to pretending Kara hadn't been strangled and mutilated by a sick murderer with a vendetta against her for helping put away a serial killer. Her voice shook despite the significant amount of control she'd practiced over the years. "Please tell me there's a door and a lock for the bathroom."

"There is." His smile sucker punched her out

of nowhere, and Aubrey held her mouth in a tight line until she trusted herself to speak again. He didn't give her that chance. Nicholas's expression collapsed as though he'd read her mind, and he slung his duffel bag to the floor. Closing the distance between them, he reached out for her, but hesitated and pulled back. "Aubrey, this is temporary. We're going to find who's behind this, and we're going to make sure he can't hurt anyone else. Together. I give you my word. You're going to get through this."

She licked dry lips, and his gaze instantly homed in on the movement, shooting awareness through every cell in her body. He was doing this to keep her safe. She knew that, but she wouldn't be of any use here. She needed to see the photo of the second victim. She needed to help. "Agent James—"

"Nicholas," he said.

"Nicholas." She tested his name, felt the weight of it on her tongue and the flood of saliva from her salivary glands. Aubrey breathed through the burn of tears at the back of her throat. Kara was gone. Nothing would change that fact, but the agent in front of her gave her hope it was possible. Her gut clenched. No. This was a murder investigation. Her sister's murder investigation. Whatever this…connection was between her and Nicholas wouldn't go beyond professional.

It couldn't. "Maybe you're right. I'm not thinking clearly. I think I'll take a few minutes to myself, after all."

Chapter Five

Nicholas watched the medical examiner ascend the stairs, her suitcase in hand. He'd been assigned this case as he had any other in the BAU. Dealing with the victims' families had always been left for the unit's public relations liaison, Caitlyn Yang, to tackle. Not part of his job description. He hunted serials. He got inside their heads, profiled their victims in an attempt to understand what set them off, but with Aubrey...

Something urged him to follow her up those stairs and make sure she was okay, even though he knew the truth. The doc was logical, understood life and death better than anyone he'd ever met, but losing her sister wasn't something Aubrey would be able to explain away. He held himself in place. No. He wasn't the person witnesses and families turned to for comfort. He was the one who brought the dead justice.

Retrieving his duffel bag from the floor, he cleared the safe house room by room, which took all of five seconds, because it was the size of a shoebox. He deposited his overnight bag onto the sectional and unpocketed his phone. He studied the photo Dashiell West and Madeline Striker had recovered from the cargo van near Kara Flood's death scene. They were still waiting on Dr. Caldwell's autopsy results from the first victim, but he couldn't ignore the fact a second had already been killed. Discovered less than twenty-four hours apart. Whoever'd gone after Kara Flood would've already had to have killed the woman in the photo in order to leave the Polaroid in that van in front of Kara's apartment building.

Nicholas pulled his laptop from his duffel and logged in to the FBI's missing persons database. If the victim in the photo had been killed before Kara Flood, there was a good chance she'd already been reported missing. Brown hair, Caucasian, approximately five-six or five-seven. Business suit. He paused. The Gingerbread Woman had focused her retaliation on female colleagues within her law firm. If the killer who'd re-created the X Marks the Spot Killer's MO with such detail was, in fact, the same killer who'd gone after Jane Doe, he would've followed the MO to the letter. It was possible the victim in the photo was also a lawyer or worked in a law firm. He scanned the list of potential victims, singling out a woman who'd been reported missing two days ago by her mother. A woman who'd worked for a law firm in the city. "Paige Cress."

He swiped his thumb up his phone's screen and messaged David Dyson, the BAU's intern keen on following in Nicholas's footsteps, to tell him to run a background check on the potential victim.

"You found something?" Aubrey rounded into what passed for the living room and leaned against the wall sectioning off the space from the kitchen on the other side. She'd changed out of her business attire into a pair of drawstring sweatpants and a dark T-shirt. Her brown hair draped around her shoulders, and time seemed to freeze.

In all the times they'd been in the same room, he'd only spoken with her in an official capacity. Autopsy reports, pathology, cause of death. Hell, he'd even read a few books by medical examiners to be able to understand her during their last investigation together. He'd gotten used to her hair pulled back in a ponytail, the professional distance she'd kept between them with her black slacks and button-down shirts she'd worn as though they emotionally protected her as well as a piece of armor. This was…something different. She was different.

A hint of desperation rolled her lips between

her teeth. "Did you find something about Kara, or does it have to do with the other woman your team believes was murdered using a different MO by the same killer?"

"You heard my call with Agent West, did you?" He wasn't sure why he was surprised. Dr. Aubrey Flood had broken every expectation he'd had of her from the beginning. She was highly intelligent, yet more personable than most academics he'd met, including her counterpart working this case. She was sincere, warm and didn't believe herself better than anyone else. If anything, he sensed the opposite after her admission of bending herself backward for the benefit of others, how she described her job as helping the families of the deceased rather than a need for justice.

He leaned away from the laptop, not entirely sure how carefully he should tread. The good doctor had been vital in capturing the X Marks the Spot Killer three years ago, but investigating the cause of death of strangers compared to her own sister were two separate departments. "Listen, Doc, I'm not sure—"

"You think I can't handle the details of my sister's murder investigation." She crossed her arms over her small frame. Her humorless laugh penetrated through the silence settling between them before she raised her gaze to his. Aubrey pushed off the wall, shortening the space between them, and his body shot into heated awareness. She took a seat beside him. "To be honest, I don't blame you. It's hard for a lot of people to compartmentalize their emotions when they suffer a loss like I have, but I've been burying my emotions for a long time. Whatever relates to Kara's case, I can handle it."

He believed her. With an entire life of ensuring others' needs were met before her own, Aubrey had the emotional awareness of her feelings, but she wouldn't have acknowledged them in order to become the keystone of those who needed her. If anyone could compartmentalize that kind of grief, that pain, of losing someone they loved to such violence, it would be her. He turned his attention back to his laptop screen and away from the outline of her soft pink lips. He pulled up the photo forwarded from his team. "Agents West and Striker recovered a photo of a potential victim with Koko. A woman. At a glance, it looks as though she was killed using a different MO than the one used on your sister. The blue lips indicate—"

"Asphyxiation." Aubrey leaned against his arm to get a better view of the victim, and a hit of her light perfume—maybe even the same brand as the killer had stolen from her apartment—dived deep into his lungs. Something along the lines of jasmine and rose, maybe a hint of vanilla. "The victim was most likely suffocated, but I won't be able to know for sure unless I'm allowed access to the remains."

"The way she was killed fits an MO for another serial killer the press started calling the Gingerbread Woman. All the victims were attacked in parking garages at their law firm, suffocated with their jackets and left with a photograph of another victim." Nicholas splayed his fingers wide, palm up. "No witnesses. No surveillance footage. That led us to believe the killer was actually working inside the same building the victims were killed in. We were able to identify Irene Lawrence by a strand of hair that'd gotten stuck to one of the victim's jackets during a struggle. Five in all. All female, all working for the same law firm she did."

"She was leaving the photos of her victims like bread crumbs." A visible shiver chased across Aubrey's shoulders, and he drowned the urge to trail his hand down her back to soothe it. "The Gingerbread Woman was leading you to her next kill like the X Marks the Spot Killer was leaving maps for family members to find their loved ones."

"During an interview with a psychologist who was writing a book on female serial killers at the time, Irene Lawrence admitted she'd been inspired by the X Marks the Spot Killer. Just as our current killer seems to be. The only difference is, I believe whoever murdered Kara and this woman isn't simply inspired, he's re-creating the MOs of his heroes in order to prove he's surpassed them." Not simply a copycat. Something far more dangerous.

He turned the laptop toward her and switched screens back to the FBI database. "Paige Cress, a paralegal who worked for a firm downtown, fits the description of the woman in the photo and was reported missing two days ago. Given the fact her photo was recovered near Kara's apartment, it stands to reason she was killed before your sister in order to keep law enforcement playing the game. Does the name sound familiar? Did Kara ever mention a friend who worked in a law firm or have reason to reach out to a lawyer? Maybe they were friends?"

"No. Not that I can remember." Aubrey shook her head. Distance swarmed into warm eyes that urged him to get closer. "As far as I knew, most of her friends were other teachers from her school, and as I said before, she rarely went out."

"I have our intern, David, running a background check on Paige to see if there are any other connections." He studied the photo once again, searching for any detail that might give them an idea of where the remains had been left.

The killer was playing with them, and Nicholas couldn't see the endgame—not yet—but that didn't unnerve him as much as the mesmerizing woman beside him. He scrubbed a hand down his face. One fact they could rely on: Paige Cress's remains would be another piece of the puzzle. One that would lead them either to the next victim or to the killer.

"The body was disposed of on top of what looks like worn wood, possibly a dock or a pier, but that's not enough to narrow down a location given Seattle is one of the largest coastal cities in the United States. There are hundreds of docks and dozens of piers."

"You said he's a narcissist. That's why he left Kara's body in such a public place, so he could show off his handiwork. It's about pride for him, and a need to be recognized as a master compared to his heroes. He'd want to do the same for this victim, too, wouldn't he? He'd leave her somewhere busy enough no one would be able to pinpoint when the body was dropped or give a credible ID. Maybe a dock or a pier that gets a lot of foot traffic."

She circled the photograph on the screen with her index finger. "This wood is distressed, as though it's been exposed to salt water for years. Assuming the victim has been kept within the city limits, only battering winds, tides and rains, most likely from a large enough source such as Puget Sound, would've been able to age the dock like this." She latched her hand on to his forearm, and a shot of heat bolted up through his veins. "The waterfront. The city had to close down one of the piers due to it shifting away from land last month. They're not scheduled to make repairs for another few weeks, but the piers on either side would still be open to the public."

She was right. Nicholas reached for his phone and hit Madeline Striker's number. Raising the phone to his ear, he nodded toward the stairs as the line rang. Her logic made sense. "I'll call it in. Grab your gear. We need to find that body."

EXHAUSTION PULLED AT her ligaments and muscles as she stepped out of Nicholas's SUV. Waves of heat gave the illusion of a dreamlike state across the pavement and long stretch of Puget Sound. One of the few thunderstorms of the summer had begun its approach from the north, dark clouds forming a few miles off the coast, and had cleared out most of the tourists and waterfront visitors. Despite the stereotype of Seattle's weather patterns, the city didn't see as much rain as most of the people in the country believed, but when the storms hit, they hit hard. And looking at the formation of clouds out across the sound, the BAU had a limited amount of time before the victim's remains might be compromised.

Another SUV parked beside them as Aubrey rounded the hood to meet Nicholas, and the two agents she'd noted at the crime scene this morning exited the vehicle. Agents West and Striker. She didn't know much about the male agent experienced in cybercrimes, with only a few short interactions between them over the years, but Agent Striker had been quite useful in searching for serial victims over her career within the BAU. Without the missing persons expert, Aubrey doubted they would've recovered a number of victims before their killers had finished what they'd started.

She nodded to both of the agents and slid her hands into her slacks, feeling more out of place in the field than in her examination room. With its drains, exposed pipes, surgical instruments and refrigerated drawers, she felt in control there. This… This was something else. She wasn't an investigator. Not the kind that followed the clues, put the pieces together and saved the day. Not like Nicholas. The victims she dealt with on a daily basis came to her already deceased, but the guilt taking root inside, the kind that blamed her for what'd happened to Kara, wouldn't let her go back and hide in her comfort zone. She owed it to her sister to find whoever killed her.

Nicholas brushed against her arm, resurrecting that flare of heat and disorientation as he had back at the safe house. "Storm's moving in. I figure we've got about twenty minutes of search time before things get real complicated."

Heavy rains washed away evidence. If they didn't move fast enough, they could lose anything that might identify the next victim or the killer.

"Where do you want us?" Agent West's incredibly brown eyes flickered to her for the briefest of moments, telling her far more in that single instance than she'd asked for. He didn't approve of her being involved in the search or the investigation, and she didn't blame him.

She'd been trained in pathology and uncovering cause of death. Until they recovered a body, she didn't understand what she could contribute here.

"Our unsub wouldn't have left the body to be recovered by anyone other than the people he intended to find it. That's why he left us the photo at Kara Flood's death scene." Nicholas pulled his phone from his pocket and turned the screen toward his team, every ounce the lead case agent she believed him to be. Authoritative, in control, unrelenting.

"I believe this is the woman we're looking for. Paige Cress, a paralegal for a firm downtown, who fits the Gingerbread Woman's victim pro-file. He's using the bread-crumb MO to draw us in, possibly into a trap. Dr. Flood and I have narrowed down a possible dump site on Pier 58. She and I will search there, but we can't risk narrowing our focus. West, you take the pier to the south. Striker, the pier to the north. Gear up and keep in radio contact."

Nicholas backtracked to the rear of his vehicle, West and Striker doing the same. He pulled a Kevlar vest over his head and strapped in, then unholstered his weapon, released the magazine and pulled back the slider to clear the chamber. A bullet leaped from the top of the gun, and he caught it before it hit the cargo area of his vehicle. Green-blue eyes raised to hers. "You know how to handle one of these?"

Aubrey shook her head, unable to look away from the overtaxed muscles of his forearms. "No. Not really."

He offered her the weapon, the weight of his team's study burning between her shoulder blades, but Nicholas didn't seem to notice. As though in his world, she was all that existed. He set the grip of the firearm in her hand then maneuvered behind her, his mouth close to her ear. Positioning his index finger over hers, he directed the finger she'd use to fire the weapon should the moment call for it alongside the trigger.

"Safety is here." He pointed to the small button above the trigger. "Magazine release is here. You currently have fifteen bullets. To load a round into the chamber, you pull back on this slide." He brought her left hand up and set it on top of the gun. "Always use your nondominant hand to load and unload the weapon. That way you're not wasting valuable seconds switching hands. Go ahead."

She pulled back the slide and heard a distinct click that said she'd loaded a bullet into the chamber. Her hand shook. The weapon was heavier than she'd imagined it being. "Now what?"

"Now you take a deep breath before you accidentally shoot me." His laugh whispered along the underside of her jaw and sent a rush of warmth straight into her gut. His hand slipped from hers, and an instant coolness absorbed into her body from the breeze coming off the sound. Pulling what looked like another vest from the back of the cargo area, Nicholas handed it to her. "Put this on. Stay behind me. If anything goes south, you use me as a shield, then get the hell out of there and don't look back. You understand?"

His words registered through the haze his proximity had built, and all evidence of the bubble he'd created around them disappeared. "You think he's here. That he's watching the remains because he enjoys the rush of the chase?"

"This killer, whoever he is, has broken in to your apartment, targeted your sister and left a map to her remains on your apartment door, Aubrey. From what I can tell, he has an unhealthy obsession with you, and I will do whatever it takes to make sure I deny him as long as I can." He pulled a second firearm from the cargo area and reached up to the SUV's hatch and slammed it closed. He lowered his voice. "Wear the vest, use the gun if you have to, but no matter what happens, do not leave my sight." Cutting his attention over her shoulder, he called to his team, "Let's move out. That storm is getting too close for my comfort."

Aubrey attached the holster he'd handed over to the waist of her slacks and fit the bulletproof vest over her head. The weight sank hard on her shoulders and stole the oxygen from her lungs as she followed behind Nicholas and his team across the parking lot.

The Seattle Waterfront centered on an atmospheric collection of piers filled with souvenir shops, amusement attractions, an aquarium, cruise ship boarding, seafood restaurants and the Seattle Great Wheel. Gondolas overlooked Puget Sound and gave postcard-perfect views of the coastline and the city all at once. On the week-ends, the farmers market was packed with tourists and locals buying fresh produce and crafts, but as dark, swirling clouds moved in, visitors retreated to the safety of their vehicles as the BAU spread out. Agent Striker veered off to Aubrey's right, heading for Pier 59, with Agent West taking the pier to her left, leaving her with Nicholas.

She adjusted the Kevlar vest around her neck as they crossed the sidewalk clinging to the edges of the piers, the weapon he'd given her heavy on her hip. Blockades prevented waterfront visitors from crossing onto Pier 58, but Nicholas didn't pay them any attention. Following in his wake, she stepped onto the old, weathered wood that was a strong match for the wood pictured with the victim in the photograph. The combination of metal and wood seemed to groan with the addition of their weight, and her heart shot straight into her throat. "In order to keep the body from being discovered too quickly, I imagine the killer left Paige Cress protected from the elements. Out of sight. Possibly in one of the maintenance sheds."

"You're probably right." Nicholas unholstered his weapon. "We'll start there."

Her steps echoed off the planks under her feet. Cement stairs branched off the concave pier and led to the piers on either side. Movement caught her attention from the right as Agent Striker moved farther out toward the end of Pier 59. Sphere-shaped white lamps flickered to life as the clouds centered directly overhead. Spits of rain stained the planks around her and caught in her hair. The storm was just beginning. They were running out of time.

Water *tinked* against the frame of the Seattle Great Wheel at the end of the pier. There were too many man-made angles that kept them from seeing the expanse of the pier as a whole—too many places to hide.

Nicholas moved ahead of her, the muscles down his back rippling with every step as they closed in on the closest maintenance shed. Built from the same cement as the stairs, the shed had been graffitied over the years with bright red and yellow spray paint. Steel double doors had been raised enough to allow the planks to run into the space. If the killer had wanted to protect the body from being found until the right time, this would be an ideal location to keep Paige Cress to himself until he was ready to show her to the world. Nicholas tested the handle, and the door swung open.

"Holy hell," he said.

Hot waves of decomposition and baked flesh dived deep into her lungs, and both she and Nicholas stepped back to release the buildup of bodily gases. The outline of a body registered as her senses adjusted to the darkness inside. Aubrey crouched alongside the remains, her medicolegal kit thudding against the pier. "Female, approximately twenty to twenty-five years old, which falls into the description given of the victim. There is evidence of petechial hemorrhages in the face, edema in the fingers and blue discoloration of the skin, suggesting the victim died of asphyxiation." Aubrey memorized the face of the victim, down to the obvious perimortem bruising in her face. She pulled back, her heart heavier than the Kevlar pulling on her shoulders. "I believe we've found Paige Cress."

Chapter Six

Nicholas stared down at the remains as Aubrey performed the initial study of the body. Heat had engorged the skin around the victim's eyes, mouth and stomach, but he agreed with the ME's identification. They'd found Paige Cress.

"It'll be difficult to narrow down time of death in these conditions. Cement holds heat, which will raise body temperature, but the wood planks underneath the remains are spaced far enough apart to allow the ocean to cool the underside." Aubrey stepped back. "We won't know anything until we can get her to Dr. Caldwell to have him perform the autopsy."

The detachment in her voice as she spoke about the victim who'd been suffocated and left to play a part in a psychopath's mind game jarred him. This wasn't a body. These weren't just remains to be cut open and studied. This had been a woman who'd worked hard to land a paralegal position in one of the city's largest law firms, who'd been reported missing by a family who'd cared about her. Doubt scattered the similarities he'd noted between them. He'd spent most of his life trusting a man who'd murdered thirty women over the course of his life until Nicholas had caught the son of a bitch. He couldn't take anyone at face value. Not even Aubrey. He had to remember that.

"The killer wanted us to find your sister on that bench. He wanted us to find Koko in the back of the van. He wanted us to find the photo of Paige. He's been leaving us bread crumbs from the beginning. Taunting us because he likes the feel of the chase. Not only is he trying to prove he's better than his idols, but he's determined to outwit the investigators on his trail. This is a game for him, and he's got a front-row seat to the whole show." Nicholas unclipped the radio from his vest. "Striker, West, come in."

Static punctured through the frequency. No answer.

Aubrey searched the area for Madeline Striker. "I don't see Agent Striker. She was there a minute ago."

Warning knotted at the base of his spine. He hit the press-to-talk button again. "Striker, West, do you copy?"

Damn it. Nicholas attached the radio into place, instincts screaming. His team wouldn't have gone silent without specific instructions or a damn good reason. Something was wrong. He nodded toward the weapon now clutched in Aubrey's hand. They couldn't leave the victim unsupervised, but he wouldn't abandon his team, either. "You remember how to use that?"

She glanced down at the firearm as though suddenly aware she'd taken it out in the first place and widened her stance. "I remember."

"Good. Call this in. Don't let her out of your sight. Understand?" He extracted his phone and dialed SSA Miguel Peters. The line rang once. Twice. "I'm requesting backup, but I give you permission to shoot anybody who comes near you without official identification. I'll be back as soon as I can."

"I'll protect her." She nodded a split second before he turned his back and took the first few steps to head across the pier. "Agent James."

Nicholas twisted around, catching the full sight of her standing guard over the body with his backup weapon in hand, and his gut clenched harder than it should have.

"Be careful," she said.

The doubt that'd trickled past his defenses cracked. "You, too."

The ringing ended, and the call picked up. He pressed the phone harder against his ear. "You've reached Supervisory Special Agent Miguel Peters…"

"Damn it. Voice mail." Keeping low, Nicholas ended the call and took cover behind one of the cement columns making up the inclined roof of a carnival game booth. He shoved his phone back into his pocket and broke cover to search the pier. No movement. Nothing to suggest an ambush. "Where are you, you bastard?"

Straightening, he forced one foot in front of the other around the curve of the damaged pier toward Miner's Landing—a souvenir shop—and the Seattle Great Wheel. Muted catches of sunlight reflected off the ocean waves, the scent of salt water clearing the lingering odor of decomposition from his lungs. Gulls screeched overhead, and he looked up.

Movement registered in his peripheral vision then vanished, so fast he almost believed he'd imagined it. Almost. His heart rocketed into his throat. The shadow had disappeared behind the long stretch of the souvenir shop, and he picked up the pace. The killer didn't just want to prove he was better than the BAU assigned to take him down. He'd want to humiliate them by showing he held all the power. This was all a game, but one Nicholas was prepared to win. His legs burned as he closed in on the northeast end of the building. He pressed his back against the old wood and craned his neck around the corner, air lodged in his throat.

Empty.

Blue umbrellas adorned minimalist outdoor restaurant seating along the south side base of the Ferris wheel. Hip-height Plexiglas created a barrier that led toward the back of the building. His pulse pounded hard in his throat as he maneuvered toward the southeast corner of the building. Tourists had cleared the piers with the oncoming storm, but Nicholas still felt as though he was being watched. Air-conditioning units and storage prevented any chance of escape along the back of Miner's Landing. There was nowhere for the killer to run.

Nicholas crept past the restaurant with its gleaming windows offering perfect views of the sound and swung around the corner, weapon aimed high.

An elbow slammed into his face. Lightning exploded behind his eyes as he stumbled back. He fell into the Plexiglas divider around the restaurant seating. Pain ricocheted around his skull as he tried to focus. A hole of clarity spread, but he wasn't fast enough.

A second hit rocketed into his jaw.

Nicholas flipped over the half wall and slammed onto a glass table on the other side, his weapon slipping from his hand. Glass shattered under his weight and sliced into his fore-arms and the back of his neck. Stinging pain woke the nerve endings throughout his body, and a groan escaped his chest. He shook his head as the masked attacker vaulted over the barrier and landed beside him.

"Agent James, so good of you to join us. I was starting to worry you wouldn't get my message." The distorted voice beneath the mask grated against his inner ears. Muscular build, well over six feet, trained in hand-to-hand combat. No identifying scars or tattoos. The killer had been watching, waiting, for the BAU to recover Paige Cress in the maintenance shed.

"You've got some control issues." Nicholas hauled himself to his feet, glass crunching beneath his boots. His pulse pounded at the back of his head, and he swiped a fair amount of blood from a laceration. He struggled for balance as he faced the bastard who'd targeted Kara Flood and Paige Cress. "Where are West and Striker?"

"Always out to be the hero, aren't you, Agent James? Or should I call you Nicholas? It's not enough you took down the X Marks the Spot Killer or the Gingerbread Woman, but you have to save your teammates as well. I've always admired that about you," he said. "In a way, you and I are very similar. Each trying to rise above the circumstances we were dealt. But where you've chosen to hunt the legends responsible for so much pain and loss, I've chosen to become one. When this is over, everyone is going to know who I am, but don't worry, your teammates are alive. For now."

Nicholas struck out, fisting the attacker's black jacket, and slammed the killer into the reflective glass of the restaurant. The window cracked beneath the momentum and spidered out around the killer's head. "You don't know anything about me."

A low, steady laugh penetrated through the ringing in his ears.

"On the contrary, Agent James. I'm your biggest fan." Wrapping his gloved grip around both of Nicholas's wrists, the suspect twisted out of his hold. The pier blurred in Nicholas's vision as the killer kicked his legs out from under him and slammed him facedown into the shattered glass of the destroyed table. "You're one of the best, and I like to honor my idols the only way I know how."

A scream tore from his throat as pain unlike anything he'd experienced before burned down the side of his face. Nicholas rolled out from under the suspect's grip onto his back and kicked out hard with both feet. He landed a hit in the center of the bastard's chest and threw him backward into an adjacent table. Shoving to his feet, he pulled a piece of glass from the entry wound in his cheek and tossed it to the ground. Blood dripped from his chin. He swiped it away with the back of his hand. He spit the copper and salt mixture from his mouth.

"You honor the killers you admire by becoming them, by re-creating their kills to prove you can do it better than they did and never get caught, but, the way I see it, you're nothing more than a copycat playing dress-up."

"I am better." A hint of rage filtered through the killer's voice, and Nicholas inwardly cringed against the pain of a smile.

"Seems I hit a nerve." He spotted his weapon a few feet away. "You see, I had you pegged the moment I saw Kara Flood's body. Using another killer's MO?" He shook his head in disappointment. "What that tells me is you're a run-of-the-mill narcissist. There's nothing special about you. You're going to go down like all the rest of the killers I've put behind bars."

"That's where you're wrong, Agent James," the killer said.

Nicholas lunged for his firearm.

Faster than he thought possible, the man in the mask shot a heel out and slammed it into the back of Nicholas's knee. He hit the pier as the tendons along his leg screamed. An arm snaked around his throat, pulled him into a wall of solid muscle and squeezed. The killer lowered his mouth to Nicholas's ear. "Dr. Flood is one of the best, too, isn't she?"

His attacker strengthened his grip around Nicholas's throat and dragged him from the outdoor seating area of the restaurant. His boots caught on the old wood as he fought for dominance, but the killer had the upper hand. Pressure built in his chest as he clawed for escape. "Without her, you and your team never would've been able to identify Cole Presley as the X Marks the Spot Killer. Would you like to know how I'm going to honor her?"

No. Not Aubrey. Nicholas locked his back teeth as dizziness swirled through his head. He clutched the suspect's forearms, fighting for release.

"You see, I've been studying all kinds of MOs for a few months now, trying to get a feel for which one fits me best." The killer hauled Nicholas to the edge of the pier, the wide expanse of the bay glittering back at him. "I've got to say, I think I've found exactly how to introduce myself to the world, and Dr. Flood is going to be my masterpiece."

Darkness closed in around the edges of Nicholas's vision, just as his attacker threw him over the railing and into Puget Sound.

NOBODY CARED ABOUT a victim when they were alive, but people sure took notice once they were dead. The bruising along the victim's mandible and maxilla, combined with the cuts and scrapes along the backs of Paige Cress's metacarpals, told a clear story of an attempt at survival.

Aubrey had been instructed to stay with the body until the BAU backup arrived, but every moment the internal heat of the maintenance shed baked the remains could lead to another piece of evidence lost. Evidence that might identify the victim's killer. The medicolegal investigators would normally examine and document everything on the body before getting it ready for transportation to her office, but time was of the essence here. She holstered the weapon Nicholas had given her for protection. Wood planks bit into her knees as she dragged the death investigation kit she usually kept in the trunk of her car closer. Popping the lid, she pulled the sterile cuticle sticks from the depths along with two evidence bags and a pair of latex gloves.

She'd trained to study the causes and effects of human disease and injury in order to investigate sudden, unexpected or violent deaths. Sometimes that involved visiting crime scenes, reviewing medical records and performing autopsies, but she considered collecting evidence to be used in court possibly the most important part of her job.

Especially in a homicide. Aubrey removed one of the cuticle sticks from its container, a seven-inch piece of wood with angled tips at both ends, and curved it beneath the victim's right thumbnail. If Paige Cress had struggled with her attacker, as the bruises and contusions suggested, there was a chance she'd scratched the killer and collected his DNA under her nails.

After swiping the cuticle stick under each fingernail, one for each hand, she bagged and labeled the evidence with the black Sharpie from her kit. She secured both bags in the extra compartment at the bottom of her kit. She needed the victim's body temperature despite the fluctuations in conditions where the killer had dumped Paige Cress to be found.

Inserting the digital thermometer from her kit, she brushed the sweat dripping from her hairline away with the back of her hand. She noted the victim's temperature and the time taken. "It's hotter than a hippo dipped in hot sauce in here."

The victim's skin was already slipping out of place due to rising temperatures. She had to hurry. Swabbing the injuries on the back of the metacarpals, Aubrey bagged and tagged the evidence before moving on to collecting particulates from Paige Cress's clothing. Tweezers in one hand and a magnifier in the other, she leaned over the remains, and a hint of gasoline coming from the victim's clothing burned down her throat. Nicholas had said the Gingerbread Woman had attacked her victims in the parking garage of her law firm in order to take out the competition for promotion to partner. If the copycat who'd lured them to the waterfront had followed the serial's MO exactly, it stood to reason he'd attacked Paige Cress in a garage, too.

A guttural scream punctured through her focus, and Aubrey straightened. Her heart threatened to beat straight out of her chest as she stared across the pier for a sign of the BAU team. Instinct kicked in, and her adrenal glands triggered the release of adrenaline, honing her senses. She'd recognized that scream. "Nicholas."

He'd told her to stay with the body, to not let anyone come close to it, but the agent was obviously in pain. He might need medical attention. She replaced the tweezers and magnifier back into her kit and unholstered the weapon he'd loaned her. Waiting. Nervous energy licked up her spine, but she couldn't hear anything else. She glanced back toward the body, torn between following his order and the inner need to help. She'd collected evidence from under the victim's fingernails, noted body temperature, swabbed for injuries and gathered a few particulates from the remains. Paige Cress was already dead. There wasn't anything Aubrey could do for the victim, but she could save Nicholas. "Okay."

She pushed her kit into the cement shed with the remains and secured the door. Turning back to face the water, she sprinted across the pier toward the last location she'd seen him. Agents Striker and West would've heard the scream. They would know where to find him. The pounding of her feet against the pier reverberated up through her frame and intensified the sweat building at the back of her neck. She turned the corner leading into the walkway between Miner's Landing and the Seattle Great Wheel, pulling the weapon shoulder-level out in front of her.

Nobody was there.

Confusion rolled through her as she battled to catch her breath. That didn't make sense. She could've sworn this was where Nicholas had headed. Taking a single step along the walkway, she listened for something—anything— that would give her an idea of where he'd gone. Every second she wasted trying to find him was another second he might be bleeding out. She tightened her grip around the weapon he'd handed her. "Nicholas?"

No answer.

Warning knotted low in her belly as the sound of ocean waves lapping against the pier fought to override her pulse in her ears. Another step, then another. She followed the slight curve of the Plexiglas divider cutting the Ferris wheel entrance off from the restaurant's outdoor dining. He had to be here. Glass crunched under her shoes. Her insides clenched. Frozen, she retraced the trail of shattered glass until she located the source. A broken table on the other side of the Plexiglas divider. She studied the red stains ground into the debris. Blood. Nicholas's? One of his teammates'? From the amount of blood left behind, the wound had to be nonfatal, but that didn't settle her nerves in the slightest. The stains had created a trail of their own, and she tracked them over the divider toward the edge of the pier. The scream. Nicholas's scream. The hairs rose on the back of her neck, but she forced one foot in front of the other to follow the blood.

One hand on the railing, the other wrapped around the gun, she leaned over. And saw him. "Nicholas!"

Facedown, he swayed with the rocking of the waves and slammed into one of the pier's supports. Unresponsive. Aubrey discarded the weapon and toed her shoes off one by one. Panic clawed up her throat as she tried to calculate how long it'd been since she'd heard his scream. Two minutes, maybe three. Climbing to the top of the railing, she jumped out as far as she could in order to avoid landing directly on him. Air rushed up a split second before the water engulfed her.

Cold water shocked her nerve endings into overdrive. The waves rocked against her and tossed her to the right. Bubbles filtered up through her slacks and shirt, tickling her skin, as she struggled to right herself. Distorted sunlight beat down, lighting the first ten or fifteen feet below the surface, but she couldn't see him. She kicked upward and broke through the surface, an automatic gasp seizing her lungs. Swiping her hair out of her face, she spotted him only a few feet from where she'd last seen him and kicked her legs as fast as she could to get to him.

"Nicholas." She grabbed his Kevlar vest and flipped him onto his back. Water drained from his mouth, his eyes closed. No. No, no, no, no. He wasn't dead. She still had time. "I'm going to get you out of here. Okay? Stay with me. I'll get you out of here."

She kicked to keep her head above water and dragged him to the next support. Another wave roared before it crashed onto them and pushed her under the water. She held on to Nicholas's vest for dear life, churning in the water until the beat of the ocean let up.

They were going to make it. She had to believe that.

Breaking through to the surface, she searched

for a low section of pier she could reach to pull them to safety. In vain. The tide hadn't come in. None of the piers would be reachable for a few more hours, and the storm had churned Puget Sound into violence. Desperation coiled behind her sternum as her legs burned with exertion. The long stretch of Pier 57 seemed like miles, but she wasn't going to give up. She couldn't. She hadn't been able to save Kara from a killer. She wasn't going to let Nicholas die at the hands of the same man.

Her shoulder screamed in protest as she swam for the southwest corner of the pier. Miner's Landing had to be able to receive their shipments of seafood from the boats. There was a dock on the other side, but cutting under the pier instead of going around was too much of a risk. She couldn't take the chance of a larger wave tossing them into the bottom of the pier. Waves battered and beat at her one after the other as she struggled to stay above water. "We're going to make it. I promise we'll make it."

She spit salt water and automatically tipped her chin back to keep her head from going under the surface. Pain lightninged down her legs the harder she kicked around the corner support. There. The docks were straight ahead. She pushed everything she had left into keeping Nicholas's head back as she swam. Thirty feet. Twenty. Tears burned in her eyes. "Almost there. Just hang on."

Her fingers clutched onto the worn, cold steel of the ladder, and she pulled Nicholas close. Wrapping her arm around the front of his chest, she heaved him into her as she backed up the ladder rung by rung. At the top, she fell, taking his weight fully, but she couldn't stop. She wasn't sure how long he'd been facedown in the water. She maneuvered out from under him as an imaginary metronome ticked off in her head. She ripped both sides of his vest free and hauled it over his head. Centering the base of her palms over his breastbone, she interlaced her fingers and administered compressions. "One, two, three, four…"

She pinched his nose and pressed her mouth to his. Salt exploded across her taste buds. No response. Counting off again, she repeated the compressions and filled his lungs. "Come on, Nicholas. Breathe!"

His chest jerked under her hands, and water spewed from his mouth as she rolled him onto his side. Nicholas's groan filled her ears, and relief washed through her. He was alive. He was going to make it.

Aubrey ran her fingers through his hair. "It's okay. I'm here. I'm going to get help, okay? Just stay with me, Nicholas. Stay with me."

"Hello, Dr. Flood," an unfamiliar voice said from behind.

Agony ripped across her parietal, the momentum slamming her into the dock. She stared up into the storm. Nicholas's hand pressed against hers, but she couldn't move, couldn't think.

The dark outline of her attacker blurred as he positioned himself over her. "I've been waiting for you."

Chapter Seven

Stay with me. Just stay with me.

Aubrey's voice echoed in his head. He blinked against the onslaught of rain. The soft lapping of waves reached his ears, gulls calling to each other overhead. Old, splintered wood caught against his skin as he raised his head. He was soaking wet. "Aubrey?"

The right side of his face and the back of his head stung as he pushed to sit up. He was on the docks, but the last thing he remembered... The killer had started dragging him toward the edge of the pier. How the hell had he gotten down here? Nicholas pushed to his feet, every nerve ending in his body on fire. He gripped the hand railing to haul himself up the stairs. He could've sworn that'd been Aubrey's voice in his head, but he'd given her strict instructions not to leave the victim alone.

Wood protested under his weight as he limped across the dock toward the stairs leading back to Pier 57. His head pounded in rhythm to the waves growing choppier with the increasing winds. Rain mixed with the blood coming from the lacerations on the back of his hand and tendriled in dendritic patterns along his forearm. He bit back the groan working up his throat and retraced his steps toward the outdoor seating area of the restaurant. Shattered glass, blood evidence—the memories of the struggle between him and his attacker revived the headache at the base of his skull.

Striker and West were still missing. The bastard had gotten to them first, but they hadn't been the killer's initial target. He'd just wanted Nicholas out of commission.

Dark shapes materialized in his peripheral vision, and Nicholas bit through the pain running down the right side of his body to get a closer look. The pair of dark women's flats hadn't been there during the struggle. He would've noticed them. A second shape took form through his distorted vision and cloud cover above. A gun. The gun he'd loaned her. Nicholas twisted his gaze over his shoulder, toward the maintenance shed where he and Aubrey had recovered the remains. "Aubrey."

Holstering the gun, he pushed himself through the pain. He sprinted across the walkway between Miner's Landing and the Great Wheel and backtracked around the corner where he'd first noticed the killer. Lightning flashed overhead, lighting his way, before thunder punched through him. The storm had arrived, brutal and demanding. Wet, uneven planks threatened to trip him up as he raced to the maintenance shed. The doors were closed, and he slammed into them palms first. Ripping open the heavy steel, Nicholas ignored the crash of the handle against cement, his heart in his throat.

The victim was still here. The ocean churned in agitation beneath the body, sea levels rising with the battering storm. In a few minutes, salt water would break through the planks and compromise any forensic evidence that might lead to their killer. A black tool kit sat a few inches from the victim. A forensic kit. Aubrey must've started collecting samples from Paige Cress, then locked the body and the evidence inside the shed to keep them secure. Why? Why would she leave the remains?

Realization hit.

Because he'd screamed. Aubrey had been with him. She'd come to his aid, armed with his backup weapon, in order to help, and must've spotted him in the water. She'd jumped the pier's railing and gotten him to safety at the risk of both of their lives. She'd saved him. She'd pulled him onto the docks. He rubbed his chest for the source of the ache under his sternum. Chest compressions?

Stay with me, Nicholas.

Then the killer had come for her. Nicholas searched the pier, thick sheets of water blacking out sound beyond a hundred feet. Streetlamps flickered but wouldn't do a damn bit of good. She was out there—alone, afraid—and he hadn't seen the threat coming soon enough to stop it.

He didn't have time to secure the victim or the forensic evidence Aubrey had collected. His team needed him. Aubrey needed him. Sealing the maintenance shed, Nicholas ensured the gun he'd loaned to the medical examiner was still loaded. The rising water levels guaranteed the loss of the evidence the killer might have left on the body once the shed flooded, but when it came to saving an investigation or saving his team, it wasn't a choice. He loaded a round into the barrel and headed toward Madeline Striker's last known position.

The Seattle Aquarium stretched the length of Pier 59, with the outdoor exhibits bleeding over onto Pier 60. Over twenty different areas and over a mile of waterfront to search. Nicholas didn't have time to waste. He tested the front door of the aquarium, surprised the double glass doors swung open. The area had been evacuated due to the incoming storm. No one should've been able to get inside the building. He stepped inside, instantly encased in glowing, blue light from the wall of glass and water to his right. Countless species of fish, coral and plant life swayed with the rocking motion of the water within the tank. The killer had lured them into his trap with the promise of another victim. He'd planned to take them out one by one to isolate his real target: Aubrey.

Nicholas crossed in front of the massive tank and around the corner into a narrower section lit with golden light from above. The items in the gift shop, locked behind thin walls of glass, cast shadows across the floor. His clothing stuck to his skin, weighing him down as he entered the crashing wave exhibit. Roaring water splashed against the clear tunnel constructed to give visitors the perfect experience of being caught under a wave without any of the danger, and his lungs ached in response. An exit to his right revealed the intensity of the storm outside, and the lights overhead flickered. He pinched the push-to-talk button on the radio still strapped to his chest, but the device didn't respond. Fried from his time in the water. He checked his pockets. No cell phone. "Damn it."

A quick search of the rest of the main building revealed neither Striker nor West, but the son of a bitch who'd taken them out couldn't have gotten far. Not when he'd had a much better target in mind. Rain battered against the door leading to the other half of the aquarium. The outline of the massive underwater dome on the other side of the pier materialized through the watery streaks against the glass, and Nicholas's instincts prickled. The killer was about proving he was better than his predecessors. Deadlier. More intelligent. Dangerous. He wanted the attention he believed he deserved. What better location to expose two BAU agents than the most popular enclosure on the pier?

He shouldered through the door and onto the walkway separating the outdoor area from the main building. Protecting his face against the violent waves cascading over the pier's railings and across the wooden planks, he sprinted for safety and down the steps into the underwater dome exhibit. The roar of the ocean died as he slammed the door closed behind him. The surface of the water visible through the grid-like construction around the dome churned faster with the intensity of the storm, but the creatures closing in on the glass showed no signs of panic. Shadows shifted across the floor as he descended deeper into the exhibit, weapon raised.

Warning climbed his spine as he stepped down into the lower level of the wraparound viewing point. The lights flickered once again then died, throwing him into a dark underwater world full of surprises and threats.

A moan reached his ears, and Nicholas turned to his right. He couldn't see a damn without the overhead lights and planted his hand against the cold glass keeping thousands of tons of water from crushing him to death to guide him. His eyesight adjusted to the shadows in slow increments, every sense he owned heightened to compensate. Heart thudding at the base of his neck, he recognized an outline against the inner wall of the viewing area. Unmoving. "Striker!"

Holstering his weapon, Nicholas dropped to one knee and patted the agent's frame for the tactical flashlight she'd clipped to her vest earlier. His fingers brushed over cool metal, and he hit the power button. The beam cast straight into the floor beside the missing persons expert but gave him enough light to see the sticky trail of blood running along one side of her face. Madeline's hands had been secured to the railing above her with zip ties. He wedged her chin between his thumb and index finger. Rich, dark eyes reflected the flashlight's beam, her pupils constricting in response. "Striker, can you hear me?"

"James…" The muscles in her throat flexed as she swallowed. "It was an ambush. He attacked me from behind. He knew we were coming."

"I know." Pulling the blade still strapped in his ankle holster, one of the few things he'd hadn't lost at sea, he straightened to cut through the ties around the agent's wrists. "Where are West and Dr. Flood?"

"He already had Dash when he secured me to the railing. He's over there. I tried to stay conscious, but…" Motioning with her chin up the stairs, she rubbed the inflamed skin around her wrists close to her chest. "Dr. Flood was with you."

A deeper groan punctured through the darkness.

"We got separated after we found Paige Cress's body." Nicholas hiked up the three steps to the main level of the underwater dome and caught sight of West zip-tied to another section of railing. Crouching in front of the cybercrimes agent, he cut the ties around West's wrists and caught him before he slumped to the floor. Striker moved into his peripheral vision, and the crush of failure to protect his team—to protect Aubrey—pulverized what confidence he had left. "The bastard took her."

"You think she's the reason the killer lured us here? That he's picking us off one by one to get her alone?" It was as though Striker had read his mind. She pulled West's head into her lap and smoothed the blood from his temple. The tough yet compassionate missing persons expert had gone out of her way to keep her emotional distance from others, but when it came to the BAU and the people she cared about, he trusted Striker to do whatever it took to protect them. She handed him her flashlight. "Go. He took our phones, but I'll get West back to the SUV and call this in over the radio. Find Dr. Flood. If she's the one he wants, then she needs you to have her back."

Nicholas headed back toward the main doors and out into the storm. "He can't have her."

IT WAS HARD to breathe.

Aubrey gasped as pain pulled her from unconsciousness. She jerked against the binding around her wrists and ankles, and the sound of chains hitting against one another echoed in her ears. Pressure built in her head and intensified the ache in her chest, like all her organs had been shoved up inside her chest cavity. She forced her eyes open and was immediately blinded by the bright light aimed at her face.

"Absolutely perfect," he said. "Just like your sister."

That voice. She recognized it from the docks, before her attacker had knocked her unconscious. Disorientation messed with her head, and she realized she'd been hung upside down. Cracks in the cement floor had been stained red beneath her. Aubrey tipped her chin toward her chest, studying the large, sharpened hook between her bare feet. The kind used in slaughterhouses. Fear clawed up her throat. Gravity battled the angle of her head, and she relaxed back into position. Her wrists had been secured before she'd been hung upside down. There was no escape. "You killed Paige Cress. You killed Kara."

"They were perfect, don't you think, Dr. Flood?" Footsteps echoed off the cement from behind. "It took me years of studying the X Marks the Spot Killer to get the marks he left on his victims' cheeks just right. You might think carving something as simple as an *X* would be easy, but you use too much force and the blade perforates the masseter muscle. Use too little and you don't get your point across."

The man in the mask stepped into her line of vision, hints of salt and sea diving deep into her lungs. Dim lighting came through a boarded and dirt-crusted window to her right, but it was nothing compared to the reflection of the spotlight from the blade in her attacker's hand. A nearby table registered. One he'd lined with surgical instruments. "I prefer a more human touch."

Masseter muscle. Most people who hadn't gone to medical school or studied anatomy would call it the cheek, but the killer seemed to have a medical background. When this was over, the BAU could use that information to narrow down possible suspects. Aubrey swallowed through the tightening in her throat and chest. When this was over...

She tugged at the zip ties around her wrists again. Nicholas had said this was a game to the killer, a show for him to get the attention he wanted from the public. Whoever'd killed Kara had fed off his victims' fears. He wanted them to know he had power over them and that he could use that power at any time. He wouldn't kill her quickly. He'd get more satisfaction from a slow kill, and that alone gave her hope the BAU—Nicholas—would find her in time. She just needed to keep the killer talking, give him a reason to talk about himself like any narcissist enjoyed. "Kara and Paige. They weren't your only victims. How many others have there been?"

"Patience, Dr. Flood," he said. "We have more than enough time to get to know each other."

"You must have a process of choosing who will become one of your masterpieces, then. Why Paige Cress? Why Kara?" She studied the room as he circled around behind her. Hooks heavy enough to hold the weight of livestock, cement, boarded windows. An abandoned slaughterhouse. The scent of the ocean said they were still along the coast, possibly north of the waterfront where he'd abducted her. In the warehouse district.

"Ah, beautiful, beautiful Paige. She had this unique habit of remembering funny moments and laughing hysterically in the middle of long silences, especially at funerals. Things no one else would remember or would think were funny." Her attacker tucked the scalpel behind his leg, out of sight as he circled her again. "She'd go out of her way to make the people around her laugh, just to bring a bit of sunshine to their day. Given the kind of work she did for one of the biggest criminal defense law firms in the city, it makes sense. She was trying to compensate for all the evil in the world, evil she helped spread by working for those lawyers. I think her outward sense of humor was her way of making up for it, but it was her smile that caught my attention the first time we met. Unfortunately, I couldn't make her my own masterpiece. No matter how many times I tried to turn her into something they would remember, she wasn't good enough for what I have in mind."

"So you used the Gingerbread Woman's MO instead." Aubrey curled her fingers into the center of her palms and pressed her knuckles together to test the strength of the zip ties. She'd been unconscious when he'd bound her, and it'd been impossible to ensure any slack in the ties, but despite what many people believed, zip ties could be broken with enough pressure. "You knew her. Paige Cress."

"Of course I knew her, Dr. Flood. I loved her." The killer stopped in front of her, cocking his head to one side. "I loved the way she talked about the books she'd read, how she'd tuck herself in at night by cocooning herself in heavy blankets, even in the middle of the summer. Sometimes, I'd watch her fall asleep through her bedroom window, and I'd get this glimpse of sadness right before she closed her eyes. The same thing happened when I suffocated her with her own blazer. You see, that moment, the one right before the light leaves their eyes, that's when you see someone for who they really are. That's when you get to know them the best."

Tears burned in Aubrey's eyes. "And Kara? Did you see who she really was before you finished strangling her?"

A low laugh shook her attacker's shoulders as he disappeared behind her once again. Pain exploded across her scalp as he fisted a handful of her hair and craned her neck back toward her spine. "I know what you're trying to do, Dr. Flood." His breath warmed against the side of her face, and she automatically flinched, but he held her in place. He smoothed his hand across her cheek. "But I can assure you, trying to get me to revel in my kills won't delay my plans for you. I chose you, Aubrey. Paige and Kara, they were exactly what I needed them to be, stand-ins until I was ready to make my own mark, but you... You're going to be my masterpiece. You're going to be my introduction to the world."

Terror increased the pain in her sinuses, and he released her. The chains holding her to the ceiling protested as she swayed away from her captor. Her plan had failed, but she wouldn't give up. She wouldn't stop fighting. "Why? Why me?"

"I know about your work with the X Marks the Spot Killer and the BAU, Dr. Flood." The killer turned his back to her, a mountainous mass of muscle across his shoulders and arms flexing as he moved. Directing his focus to the table, he studied the selection of surgical instruments as though weighing each option. "I know it was you who narrowed down the type of weapon Cole Presley had used on his victims, and I know why it was so important to you to find him."

Aubrey pressed her knuckles together as hard as she could, and the zip ties around her wrists snapped. She bit back the moan elicited by the shot of pain, and she jerked to catch the ties before they fell to the floor. The chains above gave away her movement, but she managed to keep the tie secure against her back. Her hands were free, but she'd have to lift her feet high enough to unhook the double-banded ties around her ankles. She curled her upper body toward her feet, gravity fighting against her abdominal muscles. She just had to reach her feet. That was it, and she could escape. "You've been watching me."

The man in the mask gripped one of the tools, bringing it to eye level. The spotlight bounced off the stainless steel and reflected straight back into her face. She wouldn't be able to move fast enough. Even if she'd managed to somehow curl up enough to grip the chains, her captor would reach her first, but she had to try. "Watching, learning, admiring. You devote everything to giving the families of the dead under your scalpel the answers they need. That was why you spent hour after hour trying to find a weapon that matched the *X*s on the victims' faces. You put their loved ones' needs before your own, no matter how exhausted you were or how many meals you missed. You wanted them to be at peace, and you sacrificed your own health and well-being to provide that for them. You're selfless and well-meaning, but there's a downside to sacrificing your needs for others."

The killer faced her, his shoulders slumping as though she'd disappointed him in trying to escape, and Aubrey uncoiled. He stepped toward her, the scalpel in his hand. "You believe if you give everyone you care about your complete devotion, they'll love you in return, but you know as well as I do, that's not how the world works."

Her stomach revolted. He was profiling her, just as Nicholas had done to him. Every muscle in her body burned. Her mouth dried as the truth surfaced. "You're lying. You can't possibly know that by studying me from a distance."

"You're right in a way, Dr. Flood." He took another step, slowly closing the space between them. "There's a reason I befriended Kara before transforming her into one of my experiments, you see. I couldn't get what I needed from your parents. They're getting older, they don't trust new people in their lives at this point and, to be honest, I don't think they would put up much of a fight when it came right down to it. Kara was my obvious choice to learn as much about you as I could, and she didn't disappoint in the least. Now, here we are."

Kara? Her sister had been strangled and mutilated as a tool to get to her? Bile pooled in her esophagus. "One of these days, you'll be one of the bodies on my examination table. Whatever pain you put my sister through, I promise yours will be much worse."

The killer raised the scalpel toward her neck and pressed the blade into her skin. Stinging pain sizzled for the briefest of moments before blood trickled along the underside of her chin and dripped to the cement floor. "No, Dr. Flood. I won't. Because I need you to be my master-piece."

Chapter Eight

He'd cleared the entire aquarium. Aubrey wasn't here.

The storm battered against him and worked cold straight through muscle and deep into his bones. Nicholas spun on the spot, searching for movement—anything—that might tell him where the killer had taken her. Another wave crashed against the pier and dumped almost enough water to sweep his feet right out from under him. He couldn't stay out here. The storm was only getting worse. He had to think. "Where the hell are you, woman?"

Aubrey had been the killer's target all along. That meant something, but the buzz in his head and the panic clawing up his throat were getting in the way of rational thought. He needed somewhere quiet, somewhere he could deep dive and lay out the facts of the case without all the chaos and urgency closing in. He needed Aubrey.

One touch. That was all it'd taken for her to

calm the rage and defeat he'd tried to control since learning Cole Presley had been the killer he'd imagined catching as a kid. The memory of Aubrey's fingers framing his jaw, of her honey-warm eyes staring straight into his, surfaced, and his nervous system quieted. Nicholas closed his eyes against the rage of the storm and turned his face up to the driving rain. "You couldn't have gotten far."

He recalled the fight between him and the killer, the way his attacker had moved, his voice, what he'd said. *Dr. Flood is going to be my masterpiece.* The son of a bitch wanted to make a show of introducing himself to the world. He was desperate for someone to take notice of him. No. He wanted the BAU to take notice of him, the unit that had brought down the X Marks the Spot Killer and several other serial offenders. The killer wanted to prove himself worthy, but that didn't give Nicholas a location.

Blood pulsed behind his ears, drowning out the roar of the storm. Aubrey's phantom touch chased back the deep cold flooding through him, as real as the apparitions of victims. As much as her abductor wanted to be in the spotlight, he would need somewhere private, possibly abandoned to make an example of the medical examiner, but not someplace so remote that the BAU would never find her. Sifting through his knowledge of the area, Nicholas opened his eyes and faced the storm.

Clouds rolled low over the warehouse district directly north of his position. He took a single step forward. The area was secluded, far enough from residential witnesses that might see or hear something suspicious. An old slaughterhouse had been abandoned due to a handful of lawsuits over the years. The swinery had been forced out by growing businesses around the property. It was close enough for a muscular man of the suspect's size to haul an unconscious woman on foot. "Gotcha."

Nicholas raced into the parking lot, heading straight for his SUV. He ripped open the door and collapsed inside. Within seconds, he'd started the ignition, fishtailed out of the lot and sped toward the warehouse. Hints of Aubrey's perfume filled his lungs, but they couldn't soothe the fear of what he'd find in that warehouse if he was too late. He'd already lost too many victims to killers like Cole Presley. He couldn't lose her, too. Because despite the little time they'd worked the X Marks the Spot Killer case together and her discovering her sister's body this morning, Aubrey Flood had already slid past his defenses and anchored under his skin.

The killers he hunted, the agents he'd partnered with over the years—they'd all had an agenda of their own, but not Aubrey. She'd sacrificed her own happiness, her own needs, in order to help strangers cope with their loss and to find the truth. Too many people wore a mask, pretended to be someone they weren't, but the sincere warmth in her eyes and her friendly demeanor had carved a massive hole through his trust issues. She was the light he'd forgotten existed in his line of work. From the way she used cartoon quotes to deflect the emotional turmoil she carried to the fact she'd dedicated herself to making others see the positive qualities in themselves. He'd been drawn to her almost the instant they'd met in her morgue three years ago, and there was no way in hell he was going to let her abductor extinguish that light. "I'm coming, Doc."

Rain hit the windshield the faster he pushed the SUV, the right side of his face stinging with embedded glass. The killer had meticulously planned how to isolate his prey. Whoever'd taken Aubrey was intelligent, patient and highly perceptive, and they weren't going to give up their prize easily. Nicholas slammed on the brakes as the outline of the old slaughterhouse materialized through the watery streaks in the window. He shoved the SUV into Park and called for backup and an ambulance with the radio strapped to his dashboard. Just in case. Armed with the backup weapon he'd loaned Aubrey, he pushed out of the vehicle and closed the door quietly behind him. A single door stood out among two stories of cinder-block walls and roll-top doors, but he wasn't stupid enough to believe the killer hadn't planned for an interruption to his game. He'd have to go around, come at this from another angle.

He kept low as he crossed the lot, sidearm in hand, and maneuvered around to the south side of the building. No entry points. Not even a window low enough for him to pry open. Clearing the next corner, he studied the old docks on the west side and located another door. Broken glass from a beer bottle crunched under his weight as he closed in on the entrance. Abandoned slaughterhouse with an entry to miles of open water. It was the perfect location for teenagers to test parental boundaries and escape the pressures of life, but from the thin coat of dust on the cement and the lack of footprints under the large concrete overhang, he surmised no one had been here in quite some time.

Doubt coiled low in his gut as he pressed his back against the wall. The killer could've taken Aubrey to any number of locations. If he was wrong, if he was too late… No. He shut down that line of thinking and tested the wide steel door. It swung open. Aubrey was alive. He had to believe that. She hadn't forced herself back into his life to be ripped away.

Humidity and an acid bite climbed down his throat as he stepped into the slaughterhouse. A combination of dirt, garbage and debris coated the floor in the large space. Exposed piping ran the length of the main room and groaned with the fight of the storm outside. Water trickled down along the walls from unrepaired holes in the roof, but there was no sign of Aubrey. Not yet. He crept through the darkness, shadows clawing closer, hiding corners and ambush points. Dozens of cement columns supported the failing structure, but it was the rusted machinery and lines of stalls that held his attention. Structured with drains, heavy machinery meant to dispose of livestock, and privacy, this place was the perfect location to dispose of a body.

A hard thud echoed in his ears from the far side of the building, and Nicholas froze.

"You're not supposed to be here, Agent James." The voice bounced off the walls, became part of the shadows. Footsteps reverberated through the darkness, each seemingly coming from a different direction. "You're too late. Dr. Flood is already mine, and there is nothing you can do to save her."

His stomach soured. No. Not possible. He was going to find her. He was going to take her home.

Nicholas couldn't see a damn thing in here, but using his flashlight would only give away his position. "Why don't you bring her out here so I can ask her myself?"

The killer's low laugh reached his ears.

A hand shot out and wrapped around his weapon. An elbow connected with the sensitive tissue in his right cheek, and Nicholas stumbled back. The glass still embedded in his face screamed from the impact, but it wouldn't stop him from reaching Aubrey. The outline ahead of him separated from the shadows. Nicholas launched forward, securing the bastard with both hands, and rocketed his forehead into the killer's face. He tossed the man in his grip back into a large piece of machinery designed to haul livestock to the other side of the warehouse. "That's for forcing her to be the one to find her sister's body, you sick son of a bitch."

Dim sunlight penetrated through the boarded windows. A flash of a blade was all the warning he got as the killer struck out. Nicholas dodged the initial strike, but his boot caught on a piece of piping discarded on the floor, and he went down. Pain shot up through his back and elbows as his attacker arced the blade down fast. Catching the killer's wrist mere inches from where the tip of the knife threatened to carve into him with one hand, Nicholas used his other to search for his weapon. His fingers brushed against solid metal a few feet away. A pipe. He latched on to the heavy tool and swung as hard as he could. The crunch of flesh and steel registered in his ears as the suspect rolled off him with a groan. Hiking one leg over the killer, Nicholas rolled to position himself above the man in the mask and raised the pipe. "Where is she? What did you do with her?"

The killer swiped his leg up, wrapped it around Nicholas's chest and slammed him into the floor. Faster than he thought possible, Aubrey's abductor vanished into the shadows. The same low laugh pooled dread at the base of his spine as he struggled to catch his breath. "Do you know how long it takes the human body to bleed out from a nick in the exterior carotid artery, Agent James? Because Dr. Flood does."

Panic exploded through him. He shoved to his feet, clutching onto the pipe. "You cut her then left her to die alone."

"She's stronger than I gave her credit for. It'd be a shame if you wasted time trying to hand-cuff me while she might still be alive." The voice seemed farther away now, nearly imperceptible. "Ticktock, ticktock. Time is running out, Agent James."

Nicholas gripped the pipe, steel warming in his palm. The killer was giving him a choice.

Arrest the bastard in arm's reach or save Aubrey from bleeding out. But it wasn't a choice at all. "I'm going to find you. You're not going to get away with this."

The killer's voice whispered from the darkness, "I already have."

COLD.

Her hand trembled against her neck as she applied pressure to the wound. A growing puddle of blood collected beneath her, and in the back of her mind Aubrey understood the more blood she lost, the sooner she'd go into shock, but she couldn't stop fighting. Saliva thickened in her mouth and throat as she stared up at her feet, still secure with zip ties around her ankles. "You can do this."

Exhaustion seeped into her muscles and stole her energy drop by drop. Black veins bled into her vision. Her heart beat hard in her chest, trying to make up for the loss of volume. Breathing hard, she used the strength she had left to curl up, reaching as far as she could with her free hand, but it wasn't enough. Muscle exertion increased the pressure on her lungs and intensified the headache at the base of her skull. She collapsed back with her head high above the cement floor. The chains protested above. Sweat built in her hairline as she relaxed. She couldn't think, couldn't breathe, but she wasn't going to die here. She wasn't going to let her sister's killer get away with murder.

She wasn't sure where he'd gone, but she couldn't wait around for him to watch her bleed out. Blood worked through her fingers, and Aubrey closed her eyes, tried to slow her pulse. She estimated she'd lost about five percent of her body's blood supply, still well within acceptable limits before shock occurred. She had time. She just had to use it wisely and not overexert the precious energy she still had left. Forcing herself to take a deep breath, she ignored the slight uptick of her heart rate and curled as fast as she could toward her feet. Her free hand brushed against the zip ties around her ankles, but her strength left as fast as she'd summoned it.

A frustrated scream escaped her throat, and she fell back into her upside-down position. Kara's killer had nicked her carotid artery. She was running out of time. It wouldn't be fatal if she received medical attention in the next ten to fifteen minutes, but the added combination of being restrained and hung upside down accelerated her body's output. Staring up toward her feet, she tried not to let the sway of the chains distract her. This wasn't working. Without something to hold on to or someone to get her down, she couldn't keep pressure on the wound and reach for the zip ties at the same time.

The stain beneath her spread across the cement. Without the pressure against her neck, she'd bleed faster, but she had to risk it. Using both hands was the only way to reach her feet. After that…she wasn't sure what would happen. The edges of her vision grew darker, and a crystal-clear image of the agent she'd pulled from the ocean materialized.

Nicholas.

He'd faced off with the killer in an attempt to save her and lost. She'd managed to get him breathing on that dock, but that didn't guarantee he'd made it off the pier alive. Had she saved him at all? Her head and chest ached as her breathing shallowed. She had to get out of here. She had to make sure he and the rest of the BAU had survived. Aubrey released the pressure against her neck, her hand covered with her own blood. "Don't pass out."

Summoning every last ounce of strength, she forced her upper body to rise and stretched both of her hands toward her feet. Her fingers brushed the edge of the zip ties around her ankles, and with a last burst of desperation, she grabbed on to the bind. Plastic cut into the bare skin around her ankles. Blood blossomed in a straight line and trickled down under her pant leg, but a few added drops wouldn't throw her into shock. Using the zip ties to reach higher, she skimmed the solid steel hook securing her to the ceiling and clamped on. She sobbed with relief as she settled into the awkward fight of remaining upright. Blood rushed from her face and neck as she righted herself, but she still had to free herself from the hook without falling five feet onto cement headfirst.

Dizziness blurred her vision as she notched one hand above the other on the hook. "Okay. Okay." Her own words barely reached her ears as the world righted itself for the briefest of moments. She'd made it upright. She could use her weight to break the zip ties and swing her feet down. She adjusted her grip on the hook with damp palms. She climbed a bit higher and brought her knees to her chest. The edge of the zip ties angled down against the hook, but it still wouldn't break with her added weight. "Come on."

She kicked her heels down as hard as she could. Once. Twice. Groaning through the tear of skin along the outsides of her ankles, she kicked down a third time. The zip ties broke, and her fingers slipped from around the hook. The spotlight distorted as she fell, and she hit the cement. Air crushed from her lungs. The crunch of bone ricocheted around her head. Pain exploded from her shoulder, ribs and neck. A silent scream ripped from her throat as she turned onto her side, but the spasm hadn't released her lungs yet. Her stomach sucked in automatically as she battled to calibrate the damage then released.

Oxygen charged down her throat and increased the agony tearing through her right side. Another scream escaped and combined with a nerve-racking sob. She curled in on herself, careful not to aggravate the guaranteed fractures to her scapula and right sternal ribs.

Footsteps echoed off the barren walls and machinery stained with the odor of flesh and death. The killer? Straightening one arm, she pressed her palm into the floor and tried to pull herself to the edge of light given off by the spotlight. The footsteps grew louder, closer, and Aubrey forced herself to her feet. No. He wasn't going to finish what he'd started. Keeping her right arm pressed against her chest, she stumbled to her feet and leaned forward, out of the spotlight and into the unknown.

"Dr. Flood…" The voice came from the shadows.

Aubrey pushed one foot in front of the other, one hand outstretched to keep herself from running into a wall or piece of machinery. Her body hurt. She was bleeding, but she had to get away from here. She couldn't stop. Not until she found

Nicholas and the rest of the BAU. Her ears rang. The footsteps were following her, and panic clawed through her. Glancing back, she recognized the outline of a man inspecting the circle of light where she'd been hung upside down to die, but she didn't slow. Escape. Getting to Nicholas. That was all that mattered. Dim light penetrated through the dirt-caked windows and illuminated the long stretch of warehouse ahead of her. Tears burned down her face and clouded her vision, but she only pushed herself harder. She could do this. She was going to make it. He hadn't spotted her yet.

Blood pooled between her breasts the longer she exerted herself. Heightened heart rate increased the chances of blood loss, but she didn't have a choice. She wasn't going to be his masterpiece. Not like Kara. Not like Paige Cress. Her hair broke free of the tie and pasted to her face. Machinery obstructed a straightforward escape, and she wound around a massive machine in hopes she'd spot an escape on the other side. The tick of rain pierced through the thready pulse behind her ears. She followed the sound until her feet sliced through a puddle. There had to be an exit here somewhere. Anywhere. The roll of thunder seemed louder now, and a breeze wrestled to cool the sweat beading on her face. She was almost there. She could feel it, but her body had consumed the last bits of adrenaline. She was going to go into shock from blood loss and physical trauma.

The room tilted to one side, and Aubrey slowed. She was as dizzy as a merry-go-round manatee. A laugh escaped past her lips. That had to be one of her best quotes. Falling into the wall on her uninjured side, she forced one foot in front of the other until she cleared the door leading out onto the back docks of the slaughterhouse. Relentless wind pushed her hair away from her face, and she clutched the cold steel of the railing leading down the ramp. Puget Sound protested against the raging storm, spitting salt water into her face. The shock to her nervous system cleared the fatigue pulling her down, but she couldn't go any farther as the light-headedness intensified.

She just needed to rest for a minute. Using the railing for balance, she slid to the ground and pressed her head against the vibrating metal. Her eyes fell closed as she clutched her right side with her uninjured hand.

"Aubrey," he said.

Instant anxiety flooded through her, but she recognized that voice. Alert, insightful, soothing, it slid through her and chased back the fear knotting in her stomach. She tried to open her eyes to see Nicholas for herself, but she was so tired. She couldn't run anymore, couldn't hide. The killer was going to find her. He was going to turn her into his masterpiece. Just as he'd done with Kara.

Another sob escaped her control. She'd thought she was ready for this, that she could bring down the man who'd murdered her sister. She'd tried to save Nicholas. She'd tried, but it hadn't been enough. She hadn't been enough, and now she was alone.

Strong hands secured her against a wall of warmth, and she struck out, kicked, screamed, but the pain from the fractures in her scapula and ribs limited her motion. "No!"

"Aubrey, it's me. It's Nicholas. I'm here. I'm not going to hurt you. You're safe. He can't get to you now." The warmth disappeared, and she curled into the corner where two sets of railings met. He set something soft into her hand. "I promise not to touch you, but I need you to apply pressure to the wound on your neck. I won't touch you. I'll just wait with you until the ambulance gets here."

"Nicholas?" Was this real? His dark outline distorted through the batter of rain and dizziness. That intense green-blue gaze cleared through the haze, and then there was nothing.

Chapter Nine

Fractured shoulder blade. Two fractured ribs. Fifteen percent blood loss and a mess of stitches at her temple. Dr. Aubrey Flood had been through hell and survived. Nicholas wasn't sure how, but she'd escaped being hung upside down and drained of blood in that slaughterhouse with mere minutes of consciousness left, and he'd nearly been too late.

He memorized the pattern of bruising across the left side of her face as she slept through the sedatives her doctors had given her. A monitor on the other side of the bed tracked her heart rate while another administered blood to get her volume back up to normal levels. Pain pulsed in his jaw from a strike he hadn't seen coming when he'd approached her on that dock. Along with the rest of him. It'd been obvious she'd started shutting down and going into shock, but he hadn't been able to keep himself from touching her.

Nicholas tried for the sixth—or was it the seventh—time to read through the crime scene report from the warehouse. They'd recovered the zip ties that'd secured Aubrey's hands behind her back and kept her anchored to the hook by her feet. A good amount of blood tested positive for the medical examiner's DNA on the patch of cement lit by a portable spotlight the killer must've brought in, but there was no sign of whoever'd abducted her. No matter how many times he'd read the report in front of him, none of it processed the way it was supposed to. All he saw was the scared, traumatized woman the son of a bitch had left behind. Lucky for him, Striker and West had made it out with nothing more than bruises and a mild concussion between them.

The killer wouldn't get another chance.

"Aren't you cuter than a chinchilla's behind?" she asked.

Setting the report on the side table, he leaned forward in his seat. An immediate sense of relief replaced the anger burning through him, and he slid his hand beneath hers at the edge of the hospital bed. Nicholas scrubbed his free hand down his face. In all the years he'd investigated serial crimes for the BAU, he'd never sat beside a witness's or victim's bedside like this, but he couldn't forget the fact she'd risked her life in order to save his. If it hadn't been for her, he would've drowned out there at the pier. He had to remember that. "Hey, Doc. Welcome back to the land of the living."

"Not sure I'm staying. Whatever they gave me is very nice." Aubrey's mouth curled slightly at one corner. Her fingers jerked in his hand, and she leveled honey-warm eyes on the spot where he held on to her. "I thought you were dead. I was trying to escape so I could save you."

His heart threatened to beat straight out of his chest. "You did save me. You pulled me from the water. My chest still hurts where you gave me CPR, but it's nothing compared to the fact I wouldn't be sitting here if it weren't for you. I owe you my life."

"You've got something on your face." A laugh rippled through her, and she groaned, presumably from the bone-deep pain of blunt-force trauma to her right side during her abduction. The sedatives had cleared any kind of filter from her thoughts and her mouth, and he couldn't deny the amusement coiling through him at the sight. "Ouch."

Awareness prickled along the right side of his face. "Yeah. See, I had a little accident before you pulled me from the ocean and gave me mouth-to-mouth. The man who took you ground my face into a broken table. Nothing thirty-five stitches and a lifetime of battle scar stories can't fix."

"Beats falling five feet onto cement. We can

trade injuries if you'd like." Her smile disintegrated, and reality settled between them. She pressed against the pressure point between his index finger and thumb, and a heightened sense of comfort pushed through him. "You were trying to stop him from getting to me. You were trying to protect me."

"Yeah, I was, but I failed, Doc. I wasn't fast enough, and he got to you anyway." And he'd have to live with that truth the rest of his life. Because there was a chance with the damage done to her right shoulder blade and ribs, she might not be able to recover enough to do her job as Seattle's chief medical examiner. If she couldn't hold a scalpel steady, she couldn't perform an autopsy. The city would replace her as soon as they found a candidate, and it'd be his fault. Her entire livelihood, her dream of helping loved ones find comfort and answers, gone. "I can't imagine the terror you went through, but I need to get a statement from you when you're ready. I've gone over the crime scene photos. I've read the reports, but there's not a single piece of evidence the killer left behind that we could use to identify him. Can you tell me what you remember?"

The laughter drained from her eyes, and the effect drilled straight through Nicholas's detachment and into his gut. "I remember his voice, but it was distorted with the mask. I don't think he was someone I knew." She pulled her hand from his. "I can assume samples from under my fingernails have already been collected, and that your forensic team has taken my clothes as evidence, but I'm not sure how much help they'll be. He wore gloves when he kidnapped me. You won't find his DNA evidence in the zip ties or on the hook, and the ski mask would've prevented him from leaving behind saliva, sweat or blood."

Defeat washed through her expression, and she raised her uninjured hand to the outline of gauze at her neck. "He cut me with a scalpel."

Nicholas sat a bit straighter. They'd recovered the collection of tools from a cart near where she'd been strung up, but there hadn't been a scalpel among them. "A scalpel. The same kind you would use to perform autopsies, right?"

"Yes. He had an entire arrangement of surgical tools, most of which could be found in my own medical kit. His hand was steady when he made the incision, which suggests he has medical training." Aubrey studied the sling keeping her right elbow bent against her chest. "I remember thinking I was going to die, and that Kara must've had the same thought while he was strangling her. I didn't want to die."

"I'm sorry, Doc." Medical training and knowledge of forensics, at least enough for the killer to know he had to wear gloves and a mask when he abducted his victims to prevent leaving behind trace DNA. That could narrow down possible suspects. Nicholas pressed an unraveling thread from the edge of her sheet beneath his thumbnail. "He won't touch you again. I give you my word."

"You can't promise that. Even if we manage to stop him from taking another victim, he made it clear I'm the one he's chosen to become his masterpiece." She shook her head, and a tear streaked down her face. "That kind of obsessive narcissism, his need to prove himself... I don't think he's going to stop until he gets what he wants. No matter how many people get in his way."

"He won't touch you, because I'm not letting you out of my sight." Determination unlike anything he'd experienced before rocked through him. Aubrey had survived what dozens of victims hadn't. "He went after one of our own, and the BAU doesn't forgive that kind of offense. I'm going to do whatever it takes to keep you safe."

"I believe you." Aubrey tried to sit higher in the bed, flinching against the pain morphine couldn't touch, he was sure. "Did you find your teammates? Are they okay?"

"Striker's and West's egos are hurt more than their heads, but yeah," he said. "They're okay, and I had our public relations liaison check in on your parents. They weren't given specifics about what happened at the slaughterhouse, but they were made aware you were injured trying to solve Kara's case. They want to see you as soon as they can, but until whoever attacked you is in custody—"

"I understand. Thank you. I'm not sure how I would've managed to explain everything to them." She scrubbed her uninjured hand down her face. "Were your forensic techs able to test the samples I took from Paige Cress's remains or find something I missed on the body?"

This was where his choices would threaten a conviction once they caught up to the killer. Paige Cress's background check hadn't revealed anything or anyone that might've contributed to her death, and Cole Presley's every move had been accounted for by the warden of Washington State Corrections. "No. The storm... I didn't have time to secure the remains after I realized you'd been taken. By the time CSU arrived on the scene, the ocean had risen enough to compromise any evidence the killer might've left behind and destroy the samples you'd collected. Dr. Caldwell is performing the autopsy as we speak, but I'm not sure how much survived the storm."

"You chose to compromise the evidence and come after me?" Shock wound through her words and bled into her expression. "There could've been something on her body to give us an ID.

You could lose your job for failing to secure the remains in a homicide investigation."

"I was willing to take the risk. We're going to nail the son of a bitch, Doc." He maneuvered to the edge of his seat, forcing her to look at him. "Sooner or later, that ego of his is going to force him to make a mistake, and when he does, you and I will be there to take him down. You're right. He's not going to stop. His confidence is growing, and he'll try again."

"Why? Why would you do that?" The muscles along her jaw clenched. "You had the chance to stop him."

"Because your life was worth more than losing the chance to stop him, and if I was put in the situation again, I'd make the same call." Didn't she understand that? The minutes between when she'd vanished and when he'd found her on the docks behind the slaughterhouse had been the worst of his life. Worse than discovering the X Marks the Spot Killer had lived next door to his family his entire life. Worse than seeing Kara Flood strangled and mutilated in front of her apartment building. If he'd lost her…there wouldn't have been any good left in the world. "You're more important to this investigation than you realize. I couldn't let him have you."

"I'm a pathologist. I'm not even allowed to investigate the victims in this case. I was expendable, and you…" She darted her tongue across her lacerated bottom lip, and his attention homed in on the small change. "You were brave to face him. You saved me. I'm not sure I could do much more than say thank you."

"You might not be allowed to perform the autopsies for the victims in this case, but that doesn't mean you're expendable." Nicholas soothed circles into the back of her hand. A deep-rooted shift crushed the air from his lungs as the truth surfaced. He'd gone out of his way to detach himself from the killers and victims in his past cases, but the idea of losing the woman in front of him had triggered a change of emotion he couldn't explain. He'd made a call. He'd let the killer slip through his fingers and the evidence be compromised, but in a career where he'd seen nothing but blood, violence and death, Aubrey had reminded him there was still good in the world. How could he have let that be destroyed? "Not to me."

NICHOLAS HELPED HER INSIDE, motioning her through the safe-house door.

The days had never slipped through her fingers as quickly as the past forty-eight hours. Pain pulsed along her right side as Aubrey stepped over the threshold. Fractured scapula, two damaged sternal ribs and most likely the end of her career.

Taking in the cramped, bright decor and neutral colors, she hugged her injured arm tighter to her chest with help from the sling, and the pain flared again. Nicholas's strong grip under her elbow anchored her from losing complete control, but the cracks had already started to show. Exhaustion and constant agony broke the strongest of the human race. She wouldn't be any different.

"I'll help you upstairs then make us something to eat." Nicholas scanned the small kitchen and living space down the hallway, his voice more soothing than any painkiller she'd been administered since the attack. "I'm sure you're probably tired of hospital food, so I had the BAU intern stock the pantry and fridge while we were waiting for you to be discharged."

She nodded, not really sure what she was supposed to say, how she was supposed to react. A vicious killer had tried to kill him and two of his agents then abducted her, hung her upside down by her ankles and nicked her artery to watch her bleed out. If it hadn't been for Nicholas, if he hadn't confronted the man determined to turn her into a masterpiece, she wouldn't have walked out of that slaughterhouse alive. "Thank you."

"You're safe here, Doc," he said. "Dr. Caldwell

has Paige's and Kara's remains, and my team is going through the evidence from the scene as we speak. We're going to catch the bastard who did this to you."

"I know." Because the alternative meant living in fear for the rest of her life. The killer had studied her, chosen her. She might've gotten away from him once, but that didn't mean he wouldn't try to finish what he'd started.

They took the stairs together, Nicholas's hand never leaving her arm, and rounded into the first bedroom on the left. She caught sight of her overnight bag on the end of the bed. Everything looked exactly the same as when she'd left it to help Nicholas and his team recover Paige Cress's body, but her entire world had been ripped away from her. Pressure built behind her sternum as his hand slipped from her arm, and an instant cold flooded through her as though she'd needed his physical contact to hold herself together.

"I'm going to make us something to eat." Green-blue eyes—the same color as the water he'd nearly drowned in—settled on her, and her self-confidence waned. "You'll be okay here?"

The scrubs the hospital staff had given her after the forensic unit had taken her clothing for evidence chafed against her oversensitized skin. She wanted nothing more than to change into her old college T-shirt and a pair of sweatpants—to find a small amount of comfort in the nightmare closing in around her—but the limitations in her shoulder wouldn't let her do it alone. Heat flared into her neck and face. Her knees threatened to give out as exhaustion pulled at her ligaments and muscle attachments. "I want to change into my own sweats, but I can't... I can't do it by myself."

Realization widened Nicholas's gaze. He threaded one hand through his messy blond hair, so different than the controlled style he'd greeted her with outside her sister's apartment three days ago. "Right. Okay. Well, Agent Striker is heading up the crime scene search at the slaughterhouse, but I can pull her off that assignment to come stay with you, if that makes you more comfortable."

"I'm comfortable with you." She regretted the words the moment they slipped from her mouth, but she wouldn't take them back. It was the truth. Aubrey wasn't sure when it'd happened. But somewhere between the relief she'd felt at knowing he would be the agent to take the lead on her sister's murder investigation and realizing he was the one holding her on those docks after her escape, a life-altering connection had formed. "It won't take much. I mostly need help changing out of this scrub top and getting my arm through my shirt. I can change into my sweatpants myself."

"I can do that." Nicholas reached for her luggage and laid it flat before unzipping the main compartment. He pulled her dark gray, oversize T-shirt from the top and set it on the end of the bed then did the same with her sweatpants. Facing her, he closed the distance between them, and her pulse rocketed into her throat. "Now what?"

"You'll have to remove the sling without jarring my arm." She peeled back the Velcro supporting her thumb and unclipped the mechanism that would give her access to the inside of the sling. Her breath shallowed as hints of his aftershave filled her lungs. Salty and comforting. He must've gotten a shower during his hospital stay. She braced as he slid his hand under her injured arm and helped her lift it out of the sling. Her heart beat hard behind her ears as Nicholas brushed against her hip. The clips around her opposite shoulder and midsection released with his help, but the pain never returned. "I need help taking my shirt off."

"I usually have to convince a woman to say that to me." His laugh tunneled past the tension and warmed parts of her she hadn't realized had gone numb since the last time she'd let a man get this close. Nicholas maneuvered her uninjured arm through the sleeve of the scrub top and pooled the fabric on the side of her neck before circling around to her other side.

"I doubt you've had to convince a woman of much of anything." Cool air slid across her stomach as he slipped the shirt over her head and wound it gently down her arm. Exposed in nothing more than her sports bra and scrub pants, Aubrey shivered against the inferno coiling in her gut, and another layer of emotional control stripped free.

He collected her T-shirt from the bed, one hand still supporting her arm, and reversed the process until the hem brushed against the tops of her thighs. So careful. "I tell people I'm an accountant."

"What?" A laugh escaped past her lips. "Why?"

"As much as people claim they love true crime and want to hear all the gory details of my job, facing the real thing is entirely different, and definitely not that romantic. But nobody asks an accountant questions about their job." Nicholas flashed a crooked smile as he secured her sling back into place. "All set, Doc."

"Thank you." She let her sling take the weight of her arm and turned to sit down on the end of the bed. Her energy drained as she filtered through the adrenaline-driven haze of the past few days. "I tell my dates I'm a pediatrician. Although it's been a while since I've had to use it."

He hauled her luggage off the bed and set it on the floor near his feet as he took a seat beside her. The mattress dipped under his weight, his arm brushing against her left side, and the lingering numbness of the painkillers her doctors had prescribed vanished. All she felt was him. "You mean autopsies don't make great pillow talk?"

"Not exactly." A humorless laugh bubbled to the surface. Aubrey picked at one of the threads unraveling from the hem of her old university shirt. Silence solidified between them, and the hollowness she'd pushed off since leaving the hospital charged forward. Twisting her gaze up, she studied the lacerations across Nicholas's face from his fight with the killer, and her gut clenched. The hospital staff had done a great job of stitching the wounds, but he'd be left with permanent scarring for the rest of his life. She'd spent her career and her personal life trying to help as many people as she could—Kara, her parents, the families who'd lost their loved ones—but right then, she needed someone to help her. Tears burned in her eyes as her control fractured. "I can see him when I close my eyes."

Nicholas slid one hand into hers, rough calluses catching on her skin. "I know."

"I can hear his voice. I can hear his excitement after he cut me and feel the fear suffocating me faster than I was bleeding out." Embarrassment and shame exploded from behind her sternum, and she sniffed, turning her attention back to her lap. "I know your job is to find the killer. Trauma isn't part of your job description, but I need to know. Do those feelings ever go away?"

"No. They don't." He pressed soothing circles into the back of her hand, and the invisible thread of connection between them strengthened. "But it gets easier, Doc. I promise. One day, months or years from now, you'll wake up and it won't be the first thing you think of in the morning."

The muscles in her throat strained. "Was that how it was for you?"

"After a while." Nicholas nodded, his gaze confident and warm. "It didn't happen as fast as I wanted it to, but yeah, it got easier."

A sob clawed up her throat as the last grip on her control shattered, and the tears slipped down her face. "Can you…can you hold me for a few minutes?"

"Yeah." He slid his arm around her lower back and tugged her into his side. The room tilted on its axis as he pulled her down onto the bed, encircling her in his arms. He smoothed her hair back away from her face, his exhales warming her scalp. "I'm right here, Doc. I'm not going to let anyone hurt you again."

The sob broke free, racking through her as he held her. She pressed her hand over his heart, counting off the steady beat in an effort to gain some kind of control. In vain. Forcing herself to take a deep breath, Aubrey angled her head up to look him in the eyes and pressed her mouth to his.

TEMPERATURES DROPPED WELL below comfort level as Special Agent Dashiell West descended the stairs into Harborview Medical Center's northernmost morgue. Thick double doors protested on old hinges as he pushed into the surgical suite. A wall of cold lockers, each labeled with names of the deceased held prisoner inside, reflected blinding fluorescent light from above two exam tables in the center. Tables currently holding the covered remains of Kara Flood and Paige Cress. The pungent kick of decomposition hit Dash square in the chest and knocked precious oxygen from his lungs. He coughed into the crook of his elbow, aggravating the wound at the back of his head. "Dr. Caldwell."

A man, taller than Dash, raised his gaze from examining the victim Nicholas had recovered from the waterfront pier. The clear face shield protecting the medical examiner from contaminating the remains revealed a long, straight nose, thick eyebrows and smaller-than-average eyes. The pathologist's elongated, oval face emphasized the man's graying temples and five-o'clock shadow around his jaw. Dr. Caldwell was more muscular than Dash had expected for a man who dealt with the dead, standing well above six feet as he straightened.

"You must be Agent West. Please, excuse the mess." The King County medical examiner set his instrument on the steel tray beside the slab then rushed to pull the sheet at Paige Cress's hips higher. Tugging his latex gloves from his hands, he tossed them into the hazardous materials bin near the lockers.

Dr. Archer Caldwell extended his hand. "I don't usually get much company down here other than my assistant."

Dash shook the doc's hand, and the dull pain at the back of his head pulsed. He and Striker had been taken out of the game almost immediately after they'd split up at the waterfront, leaving Nicholas and Dr. Flood to survive a sadistic serial killer on their own. Wouldn't happen again. "You said over the phone you had something to show us from both sets of autopsies on the victims."

"Yes. Although I assumed it'd be Agent James who'd want to see what I've found firsthand, but please." Dr. Caldwell motioned toward the two slabs where each woman rested. "I've confirmed cause of death for the first victim, Kara Flood, as strangulation. You can see here from the dark contusions around her throat, the killer used an object about two inches in width. I was able to pull a few fibers from where the edge of the murder weapon dug into her skin."

Dash studied the line of deep black and blue bruising around the victim's throat, his chest tight. Kara Flood had been an exquisite woman before she'd died, committed to education and learning, with an understated beauty. The forensics tests from her dog had come back inconclusive. They needed something to nail the bastard before he struck again. "Fibers? The murder weapon shed fibers while he strangled her?"

Dr. Caldwell nodded. "Yes. Blue nylon. I had the forensics lab test the fibers against the leash you and your partner recovered with the dog from the scene. It was an exact match, but that's not what I wanted to show you. Do you see these two darker bruises between the edges of where the leash stopped? They're thumbprints. I believe the killer used his hands to strangle the victim first then wrapped the leash around her throat and tightened it in an effort to hide the outline of his hands, but the lacerations to the victim's face—"

"Kara. Her name is Kara," Dash said.

The killer might have wanted to erase these women's identities by trying to hide them within MOs from two separate killers, but Dash wouldn't. He remembered them. He remembered all of them.

"Yes, Agent West, of course. I apologize. It's just that in my line of work, in order for me to do my job proficiently, I have to be able to detach from the person I'm cutting open. Sometimes that's the only way I don't take the victims home with me." The pathologist bent over Kara again, tracing the pattern of deep cuts across the victim's face with his pinkie finger hovering above her skin.

"As I was saying, the lacerations to the victim's face are consistent with the injuries Dr. Flood noted while she was performing the autopsies during the X Marks the Spot Killer case, as we expected given the killer's testing of MOs. But instead of a hunting knife, whoever attacked this victim used a scalpel to carve the X into her masseter muscle."

"A scalpel. Dr. Flood's statement said the killer nicked one of the arteries in her neck with a scalpel, that he had a whole collection of surgical tools on a nearby table." Dash's focus shifted to the spread of stainless steel tools Dr. Caldwell had laid out to perform both autopsies on the victims. "Are you able to determine the killer's hand size based off the bruising around Kara's neck?"

"Unfortunately, no," Dr. Caldwell said. "Given the fact there are no foreign epithelial cells around the victim's neck, I concluded the killer wore gloves when he strangled her, which changes the shape and size of the attacker's hands. Add in the element of the leash to hide the bruising altogether, whoever killed Ms. Flood ensured we wouldn't be able to narrow down any identifying features."

Damn. This guy had been careful. "What about the injuries on Paige Cress's body? You said you were able to recover something even after the ocean water cleaned the remains."

"Yes." Dr. Caldwell motioned him toward the next table, where Paige Cress rested as though she were asleep—apart from the Y incision stitched with dark thread over her collarbone and down the center of her chest. "There's evidence of rapid decomposition due to rising temperatures in the shed where the remains were discovered, which made it difficult to determine time of death. With the addition of salt water washing the remains, there wasn't much to go off. But I can definitively tell you this victim was killed eighteen to twenty hours before she was placed in that maintenance shed on the waterfront. And you'll be happy to know, I found this between the victim's teeth."

The pathologist handed Dash what looked like a petri dish without the colored goo in the bottom he'd used in science class in high school. "My assistant recovered human tissue, but I've so far been unable to match it to a wound on the victim, and given it was found between her teeth, I suspect it came from whoever suffocated her. I'll know for certain once the forensic lab processes the evidence."

"She took a bite out of her attacker." Dash studied the tissue through the clear container. He handed back the petri dish. Dr. Flood had insisted whoever'd abducted her and hung her upside down by her ankles in that slaughterhouse had to have had medical training. Not only to keep the scalpel steady but to know where and how deep to cut her to keep her from bleeding out too quickly. "This is good. Have you worked a serial case before, Dr. Caldwell?"

"What an odd question, Agent West. No. I haven't." Dr. Caldwell replaced the tissue evidence on the same cart as his surgical tools. "I'd hoped at the time my work would've spoken for itself. I have years of experience in homicide investigations and have taught forensic pathology at the university for close to a decade." The pathologist's expression neutralized as he studied the victim on his slab. "But the spotlight shines on Dr. Flood."

Chapter Ten

He could still feel the warmth of her mouth pressed against his.

Nicholas listened to the doc's steady breathing as she slept wrapped in his arms. Exhausted from the trauma sustained during her abduction, her escape from a cold-blooded killer and the emotional implications of almost dying, Aubrey had fallen asleep in his arms the minute she'd kissed him. Hints of her light perfume clung to her ratty T-shirt, and he filled his lungs as much as possible.

He hadn't been able to sleep. Not with the updates filtering in from his team. Kara Flood's dog hadn't given up any viable evidence other than Koko's leash had been used in the attack, which didn't quite fit with the profile Nicholas had built so far. The killer had targeted the victim. Why then had he only brought the scalpel to use during the attack and not something to replicate the strangulation patterns on the X Marks the Spot Killer's victims? Cole Presley had used his favored belt on his victims. This killer had used his hands, making Kara Flood's death personal.

They had no suspect.

According to Agent West, the King County medical examiner—Dr. Archer Caldwell—had recovered a possible DNA sample from Paige Cress's teeth during her autopsy. She'd bitten her assailant before she'd died, but without someone to compare it to, they were back at square one. The clock was ticking down to the killer striking again, but he couldn't deny the sense of calm washing through him now.

"How many of your extremities are numb from staying in one position all night?" Her sleep-addled voice pricked awareness down his arms and legs, every inch of the right side of his body pressed against hers. Aubrey notched her chin higher. An upturn of her mouth countered the blood, violence and anger cascading in unending flashes of memory and cleared his head.

"Approximately fifty percent, I imagine, but it was worth it to be able to get you to slow down." Damn, she was beautiful. Even more so than he remembered from the first time he'd met her three years prior.

"I'm sorry. I didn't mean to fall asleep on you. You could've extracted yourself if you wanted to get into your own bed. I probably wouldn't have noticed." Pressing her uninjured palm to his chest, she struggled to sit up without the use of her right side and failed. She tried again and fell against him. "This is embarrassing, but could you please push me off the bed?"

"Sure thing, Doc." His laugh erupted easily as he straightened. Sliding his hands under her right hip, careful of her higher injuries, he rolled her onto her other side and pushed her legs over the edge of the mattress. "Nothing to it."

"Thank you." Aubrey hesitated to stand, her back to him. "I appreciate you staying with me last night. It probably doesn't seem like much to you, but I haven't let someone else take care of me in a long time. All my energy, everything I do, has been to help the people I care about and the families of the deceased who come in my morgue. I forgot how good it feels to put myself first for once."

His gut clenched. Nicholas pushed to his feet, studying the curve of her spine down her back. Her obsession with being needed had nothing to do with ensuring the people she cared about were happy or that their lives were made easier because of her. Demanding to be part of her sister's murder investigation didn't benefit anyone. No. To Aubrey, being needed equated to being loved. Being valuable and worthy to the investigation fulfilled her, but the consequences of giving herself completely to external sources had taken a vicious toll. He'd held her last night because he'd recognized the exhaustion and pain in her eyes. He'd held her because of her drive to be close to others. He'd held her... Damn it, he'd held her because he wanted to be the one to help her forget what she'd been through.

At no point in his career—in his life—had he felt more protective toward another person than he had the moment he'd found her on those docks. She'd been vulnerable, delirious from blood loss, physically weak. He'd sustained injuries of his own during the fight between him and the killer, but the minute he'd pried her desperate grip from the hand railing, he'd felt nothing but the need to care for her.

Nicholas maneuvered around the end of the bed. He crouched in front of her. Hands leveraged on either side of her hips, he memorized the angles of her jawline, the smooth skin of her neck. Every cell in his body tuned to every cell in hers, and the defensive guard he'd used to protect himself from trusting her crumbled. "You've spent your entire personal and professional life in the service of others, Doc. You took care of Kara. You take care of your parents. Hell, you even try to comfort the families of the people who come across your slab. I've never met someone so sincere, compassionate and patient, but there's only so much you can give before there's nothing left. It's your turn. Tell me what you need."

"You've done enough. You said I'm the one who saved your life, but you saved mine, too. You held me last night when I'm sure that's the last way you wanted to spend your time on this case." She shook her head, refusing to look up at him, and swiped at her cheeks. "I promise, you don't have to do this—"

"Yes, I do." He intertwined his hand in hers. Her tears streaked across his fingers. "Tell me what you need from me."

Her shaky inhale reached his ears, and a sense of emotional awareness entered her expression. "I need a shower and chocolate doughnuts with rainbow sprinkles and to watch some cartoons. I need my sweatpants, because these scrubs are too itchy, and to scream as loud as I can because of what happened, and I need…" She visibly worked to catch her breath, and she squeezed his hand. "I need you to put your arms around me again, so I don't feel like I'm going to shatter into a million pieces right here in the middle of this room."

Horror and a hint of embarrassment entered her expression, and she tried to pull back.

"All right then," he said. "Let's start with the shower."

"What?" she asked. "You were serious?"

"Serious as soggy underwear in the spring-time." Nicholas straightened, offering his hand to help her stand.

Her laugh punctured through the low ringing in his ears and worked to destroy the defenses he'd been holding on to since learning who Cole Presley really was. Aubrey slipped her hand into his, the bruises on the backs of her knuckles a small testament of what she'd been through in the past few days. But more than that, proof she'd survived, that she was as strong as anyone could be in her situation, and a swelling of admiration and attraction heated under his skin. "That was…"

"Worthy of a Dr. Flood favorite?" He pulled her to her feet, and she stumbled into him, her mouth level with his. A few centimeters. That was all that was left between them as she struggled to gain her balance.

"I was going to say graphic, but yes. Definitely worthy of making it into my top five sayings. I might have to use that one myself someday." Her smile accentuated the laugh lines around her nose, and he homed in on her lips. "Not sure of the context quite yet, though. I'll have to work on that."

She'd tasted of honey and vanilla last night before she'd passed out on his chest—a figment of his imagination, he was sure. Because the truth was, trauma affected people in a lot of different ways. It'd broken down Aubrey's obsession to be needed in less than forty-eight hours. Maybe his own trauma response triggered hallucinations, but the combination of her perfume and something inside told him he hadn't imagined that kiss at all. Sweet as honey, addictive as vanilla.

"Could you grab my sweatpants from off the floor for me?" She pointed to the pile of light gray material pooled at the end of the bed. "As much as I appreciate you helping me change out of my top last night, I think it's best if I manage this part myself."

"Take your time. I'll start the shower and work on getting one of the interns to deliver some chocolate doughnuts with sprinkles." He bent and swept her sweats off the floor then handed them off. Heading toward the bathroom positioned between both ends of this particular container-turned-bedroom floor plan, he ran through the list she'd given him over and over until her words ingrained in his brain. *I need you to put your arms around me again, so I don't feel like I'm going to shatter into a million pieces right here in the middle of this room.*

"I kissed you last night," she said.

His gut clenched tighter, and Nicholas hesitated halfway to the bathroom door. His boots dragged against the industrial-style carpet as he turned partially toward her. Spreading his hands wide at his sides, he tried to get the feeling back into his fingertips as she stared at him. "What you've been through… It can have a lot of different effects on a person. I understand you didn't mean anything by it. We can forget it happened and move on with our lives."

He wouldn't. No matter how many times he'd tried last night as she pressed herself against him, he'd replayed the feeling of her softness dominating him from the outside in. People weren't who they said they were. Cole Presley hadn't been the support system Nicholas had needed growing up. He hadn't been the father Nicholas wished had stuck around. Not really. He'd been a serial killer who got off on proving his power over innocent women for thirty damn years, and Nicholas had been too blind to see it. He'd taken big measures to ensure he was never fooled again, but Aubrey Flood had barreled into his life and turned his world upside down with that kiss.

"And if I don't want to forget it? What then?" She clutched her sweatpants a little too tightly at her side. "What if I meant it?"

Nicholas faced her. One step. Two. He closed the distance between them. Spearing his fingers through the hair at the back of her neck, he crushed his mouth against hers.

AUBREY DROPPED THE sweatpants and fisted her uninjured hand in his shirt, barely able to hold herself upright as he swept past her lips and explored her mouth with a primal possessiveness. He tasted of salt and man and fed into her rolling need for comfort the longer he refused to let her go.

It'd been so long since she'd let someone get this close, afraid as soon as they discovered what she did for a living they'd run in the opposite direction. It'd happened too many times before, the rejection, the hurt. But Nicholas didn't care about her career. The rough brush of his five-o'clock shadow shot awareness straight through her, and a moan slipped from her lips. He'd been willing to do whatever it took to help her work through the pain and fear clinging to her every thought. When was the last time someone had offered to help her with anything?

Her lungs struggled to keep up with her racing heartbeat, and Aubrey pulled away to catch her breath. She set her forehead against his, forcing herself to unclench her fist from his shirt. To prove she could. Fortifying herself against dragging him closer, she pressed her hand into his chest. "That was sweeter than apple pie on a Sunday."

"You say the most flattering things." His laugh rumbled up through her palm and straight through her chest. Nicholas circled his hand around hers and brought her fingertips to his lips. He kissed her middle finger, and she swore her knees gave out just a little bit. "I'm going to get that shower ready for you. After that, we can talk about doughnuts and cartoons." Stepping back, he stole the warmth simmering from his touch and headed for the rectangular-shaped bathroom planted in the middle of the open floor plan. "You're not alone in this, Aubrey. You still have people who care about you. No matter what happens, I want you to remember that."

No matter what happens? A rock materialized in the pit of her stomach. Her scapula and first ribs on her right side ached with the reminder the fractures had the potential to end her career. If she wasn't able to be part of police investigations as a medical examiner, would she and Nicholas even see each other when this case was closed? More importantly, what was she supposed to do if she couldn't help those families who needed answers? She nodded as the room started to spin. Whether from Nicholas's kiss, the physical trauma she'd sustained or the idea of losing everything she'd worked for, she didn't know. "I know."

He shouldered into the bathroom, and the sound of water hitting tile filled her ears. Within a few seconds, he'd directed her into the luxurious bathroom she hadn't expected in any kind of safe house. Least of all one made of shipping containers.

"This is…beautiful." She took in the glistening marble tile lining the edge of a massive jetted tub and climbing high above the top of the large glass-doored shower. A light gray vanity had been installed perpendicular to the tub, and she ran her free hand along the cold smooth surface. Steam tendriled through the air and settled against her neck and face.

"Not bad for an FBI safe house, is it?" He unclipped the attachments around her midsection and over her uninjured shoulder and maneuvered her arm out of the sling as he had last night. He set the sling on the counter, but his body heat had penetrated past skin and muscle. Just as quickly as he had the night before, he helped her out of her shirt and offered her a robe from a nearby hook before he wound her free from her sports bra. "Take as much time as you need. When you're done, I should have a lead on some fresh doughnuts and coffee." He turned to close the door behind him. "Black, right?"

"Right." Hesitation hardened the muscles down her spine, but she'd never felt so wanted, so…loved as she did right then. "Nicholas?"

"Yeah?" He pushed the door open wider, settling green-blue eyes on her.

"I couldn't have gotten through this without you." That truth resonated deeper than she wanted to admit, and an array of emotion washed through her. Fear, anger, desire, exhaustion, grief. It tornadoed into something unrecognizable and foreign, but she didn't try to stop it. She didn't try to control it. There was only Nicholas, her anchor. Her partner.

"You're the one who kept me from drowning out there, Doc. I'm the one who owes you." He sealed her inside as steam built around her and worked to soothe the aches of the past three days.

Her bare feet stuck to the floor as she discarded the robe he'd given her. Every ache, every shot of pain threatened to resurrect the memory of how she'd been injured. A flash of her counting the drops of blood hitting the floor beneath her lit up behind her eyes, and she automatically brushed her hand against the gauze taped to her neck. She'd faced the results of violence in her career, but she'd never come so close to winding up on another pathologist's table before. She peeled the medical tape from her skin and examined the cut underneath in the mirror above the vanity. Straight, yet small. Deep enough to puncture her carotid artery but not deadly enough to make her bleed out in a matter of seconds. Whoever had abducted her, whoever had hung her upside down by her ankles and promised to turn her into his masterpiece, had known what he was doing. He'd had surgical instruments, medical training, knowledge of human anatomy. Same as she did.

Aubrey stepped under the shower spray, reveling in the sharp sting against her scalp. Pooling a large amount of shampoo in her hand, she methodically washed the scent of the ocean and thick sections of dried blood from her hair with one hand. The stitches on her temple stung with the added chemicals from the shampoo, but the pain only managed to keep her in the moment. Red-tinted water swirled down the drain near her feet. Bruising protested under her touch as she scrubbed the evidence of her walking nightmare from her skin, and another sob clawed through her chest. The scent of lavender filled the shower. The forensic techs hadn't wanted her to shower at the hospital. She could still feel the killer's hands on her, still smell his breath. Still hear him telling her how much he'd needed her to be his masterpiece.

The skin along her forearm reddened, and Aubrey let go of the loofah.

She didn't want to be needed anymore. Everyone had needed her, and she'd let them, even when it was in rivalry with her own self-interest and well-being. They'd needed her because they'd known she'd come through for them. Her parents had needed her to check in on them throughout the week. Her sister had needed her to call her every night to talk about her day. Her friends had needed her to stop talking about her work in social situations, before they'd stopped asking to meet up altogether. The men she'd dated had needed her to lie about what she did for a living. Everyone had needed her. With the horrendous details of her job, she'd gone out of her way to make others comfortable in an effort to feel closer to the people she cared about, but she'd suffocated her own needs and identity in the process.

Grief charged in uninvited, and she slammed her uninjured hand against the tile wall. The little energy she'd tried to hang on to vanished. She sank onto the built-in bench and brought her legs to her chest. She'd given them everything without any kind of expectation of support in return and called it love. A one-sided relationship wasn't love. Expecting her to drop everything and come running wasn't love. Being needed wasn't love.

Physical relief lightninged down her spine and released the pent-up resentment and anger that'd lived in her bones for years. Nicholas was right. She deserved to have her needs met for once, and if it hadn't been for what'd happened in that slaughterhouse, she might never have recognized she'd been running on fumes at the expense of everyone around her. She'd had to think of only herself to escape. Not Nicholas. Not her parents if they'd lost another child. Not Dr. Caldwell after he would've been assigned to perform her autopsy.

Aubrey straightened and twisted off the water. She was tired of sacrificing her identity, tired of lying, tired of wearing herself out to make others comfortable. It was time she put herself first.

Drying herself as best she could with one hand, she robed slower than a sloth in South America but managed to fit her sling back into place on her own. Water from her soaked hair dampened the collar as she stepped back into the sleeping quarters. She descended the stairs, following the sounds of the television from the main living space. Familiar voices filled her ears, and she glanced around the corner to see the characters from her favorite cartoon working together to fix another toy. Nicholas had done exactly as he'd promised and gone through her list of needs. What kind of person did that?

Movement registered from the kitchen, and she caught sight of Nicholas at the stove top, a spatula in hand and an apron tied around his waist. She leaned against the wall for support, watching him, as the scents of frying oil and pastry chased back the lavender soap she'd abraded against her skin. Flour and chunks of what looked like dough peppered the small countertop to his right, and she raced to replace the nightmares at the back of her mind with this moment. "You're making doughnuts, aren't you?"

"Hey." He turned, a wide smile in place. "I couldn't pull my intern off the case for a run to the bakery, so I decided to give homemade doughnuts a try." He scooped a chunk of unrecognizable dough from the pan, showing off the blackened edges of one ring. "I've got to tell you, I've never been burned so many times in my life. Keep in mind they may or may not be doughnuts when I'm finished."

She couldn't help but laugh at the effort and crossed the kitchen. Taking his free hand in hers, she smoothed her thumb over the shiny spots of skin. First saving her life from a sadistic serial killer then taking time out of the investigation to help her work through her abduction and grief. Aubrey kissed one of the burns. She could get used to this. "They're perfect."

Chapter Eleven

"So this little girl has magical powers that make her toys come to life, and she's a doctor?" Nicholas took another bite from the warped, sugary doughnut he and Aubrey had salvaged from the mess he'd made in the kitchen. Her body heat spread through his right side as she huddled closer under the thick blanket they'd pulled off one of the beds. "Got to admire that kind of work ethic in a kid."

"She has a magical stethoscope, and don't bash my favorite show. It's cute." She picked a collection of pink sprinkles off the top of her doughnut—sans chocolate glaze—and pressed them against the tip of her tongue. "Beats all those true crime and procedural shows. I get enough of that in the real world."

"I can see that. I can also see where you get all your crazy sayings." His arm pulsed with the weight of her head pressed against it, but Nicholas couldn't for the life of himself—or for the life of the investigation—summon the desire to move. Not with the amount of doughnuts he'd eaten or the fact Aubrey had allowed him to hold her again. Hints of lavender from her shampoo and soap battled to replace the burned odor clinging to the kitchen and living room, but it wasn't responsible for the sense of calm pulsing through him. It was her. The warmth of her skin, the brightness in her eyes, the way she put him at ease and rocketed his pulse into dangerous territory at the same time.

And all this suddenly seemed a little less temporary.

That smile made him hope for more, but more wasn't possible. Not with him. Not when he couldn't trust the masks people wore for the world and lied about who they really were on the inside. Not when Nicholas couldn't trust himself.

Once they'd solved this case, he'd move on to the next, and Aubrey would go back to the morgue to examine the next set of remains that came across her slab. He'd gone out of his way to help her deal with the rolling effects of what she'd been through for the sake of the investigation and her mental health, but now... Now he'd started envisioning mornings just like this. Where she'd wake in his arms. He'd make her breakfast, and they'd watch morning cartoons together to escape the real-world violence they dealt with on the job. He'd imagined joining her in the shower, kissing her senseless and exploring the curves under her oversize sweats and T-shirt.

None of that reinforced the detachment he'd held on to after arresting Cole Presley, and an invisible earthquake rocked through him at the idea. This wasn't him, and Aubrey deserved a hell of a lot better than what he had to offer.

The past few hours had slipped by in the blink of an eye, but reality wouldn't be ignored much longer. A killer waited outside these walls, one who'd already murdered two women and had targeted Aubrey to prove he was better than the veteran killers Nicholas had hunted, and so far the son of a bitch was right. Most serials followed a set of internal rules when it came to stalking their prey, compulsions. They had to kill, and they had to finish that kill a certain way or in a certain order, but this one… He'd never seen a killer like this. Unpredictable, far more intelligent than he'd originally believed and seemingly lacking those internal values that helped Nicholas construct a profile.

There was no order to the way this killer worked. Not in his MO or victim choice. Maybe that was the point. Kara Flood had been an elementary school teacher, her sister the city's chief medical examiner, and Paige Cress had been a paralegal who'd been attacked and put in the maintenance shed eighteen to twenty hours before the first body had been discovered. Everything had been meticulously planned, but Nicholas couldn't see the pattern.

Images of toys come to life and a little girl who'd taken up being a doctor phased to the back of his mind. There had to be a connection. If the killer had planned to make Aubrey his masterpiece—his own sick introduction to the serial killing world—then the other two victims had only been the start of his plan. Who knew how many other pieces it would take to solve this puzzle?

Nicholas unwrapped his arm from around Aubrey and leaned forward on the couch. Instinct pulled him to his feet, and he crossed to the dining room table, where he'd set his laptop before he'd burned the doughnuts.

"Nicholas?" His name on her lips tightened a knot of desire in his gut and threatened to pull him out of his thought process.

He hadn't been able to do a deep dive since those panic-filled moments on the dock, but he couldn't ignore the zing of intuition driving him now. Nicholas scanned the attachments in the latest email from the team. "Striker and West sent photos from the first victim's apartment while you were in the shower. I only had a few seconds to run through them, but I think I just figured out how Paige Cress and your sister were connected. That's the pattern. You might not have known Paige directly before she'd died, but she knew your sister." He skimmed through the photos until he found the one he wanted and stepped back. Pointing at a shelf of books in the victim's apartment, he faced Aubrey as she struggled to her feet. "There."

"Those four books." Disbelief graveled her voice. "I recognize them from Kara's apartment."

The books. Damn it, he should've made the connection sooner. "What are the odds a paralegal and a kindergarten teacher would have the same collection of four true crime books? That must be the connection between the first two victims." He bent down, dragging a photo from Kara Flood's apartment beside Paige's. "Each of these books has been published in the last year. They're new, and judging by the spines' condition, I'd say they were all bought around the same time, possibly from the same bookstore."

"You think they were reading them together." Aubrey's tongue darted across her bottom lip, and she raised her left hand as though intending to cross her arms over her chest, but the sling wouldn't allow it. "He told me he used Kara to get close to me, to learn about me. If Paige Cress knew my sister, maybe he did the same thing to her."

"Stands to reason he would've had to have known her." The adrenaline surge of following a lead exploded through him. This was what he'd been trained for. This was what he was good at, taking the pieces of the puzzle and fitting them together to make a cohesive narrative. "We'll have to confirm through the victims' financials and track down the retailer where they were purchased, but there's only one reason two or more people buy the same set of books and read them around the same time. The victims could be part of a true crime book club."

"Kara never told me she was part of a book club or that she was interested in this kind of stuff." Aubrey stepped away from the screen. "Serial killers? Crime? I had no idea."

"Maybe she understood you wouldn't want to talk about it given how much you try to avoid that kind of entertainment when you're off the clock," he said. "I imagine broaching the subject with you would've been difficult for her."

"It's possible. I'm starting to realize she'd been keeping a lot of secrets from me. We still haven't determined how she was able to afford living in her neighborhood on a teacher's salary." She pointed to the screen. "Nicholas, look at the book titles."

He enlarged the images to read the text clearly on the books' spines. Son of a bitch. "*X Marks the Spot: The Hunt for Cole Presley. Not Your Average Fairy Tale: The True Story of the Gingerbread Woman* and *Eat the Darkness: Exposing the Watcher.*"

"If Kara and Paige were in a book club together, it can't be a coincidence the man who abducted me used two MOs of the same serial killers they were reading about these past few months." Aubrey circled out of his peripheral vision. "Do you think it's possible he'll kill more victims, given there's four books on Kara's and Paige Cress's shelves?"

But First, Lipstick. Nicholas recognized the fourth title from the shelves of both victims. The detailed retelling of the Extreme Makeover Killer, a man who'd given all his victims—redheaded women between the ages of nineteen and twenty-five—makeovers after he'd bound them and cut their wrists; an homage to his wife, whom he'd bound and killed after her attempt to leave the abusive relationship. Nicholas studied the illustrated stick of lipstick on the binding. The Extreme Makeover Killer had applied a bright red lip color on his victims, the same shade his wife had preferred, before he'd cut their wrists and watched them bleed out. Had the Extreme Makeover Killer been the inspiration behind Aubrey's attack in that slaughterhouse?

"It's possible he already has. The killer has

replicated the X Marks the Spot Killer and the Gingerbread MOs so far, every detail in line with the original cases, but the only reason we discovered Paige Cress was a victim was because the Gingerbread Woman left photos of her victims with a fresh kill. He used Kara's crime scene to give us that clue, but the Extreme Makeover Killer didn't leave bread crumbs for the BAU to follow."

Dread pooled at the base of his spine as Nicholas ran through the details of that investigation. "He hid his victims underground, where no one would find them. Whoever abducted you wants to prove he can kill as well if not better than his idols. He wouldn't have experimented with only two victims. He would consider it hands-on research, a test of his capabilities and a gathering of knowledge. These books laid out the investigations for him and walked him through exactly how to kill his prey."

He tried to take a deep breath, but the pressure behind his rib cage built faster. "There are more victims out there, ones we haven't uncovered. I'm sure of it."

"We need to find where Kara's book club met," she said.

Nicholas scrubbed a hand down his face. "And who else is a member."

THE BUILDING'S SUPERINTENDENT twisted the key for Paige Cress's apartment in the door and motioned Aubrey and Nicholas inside. They hadn't found anything in Kara's personal effects that'd given them an idea of when and where the true crime book club meetings had occurred, but Paige Cress might not have been so secretive. An immediate wall of sunlight spread across the light brown flooring and beckoned them into a long hallway expertly furnished with a bench, hooks for jackets and cubby holes for shoes. The super offered Nicholas the key. "Paige was a good tenant. Never late with rent, always greeted me with a smile. Have you contacted her family to let them know what happened?"

"We have someone in the bureau who's keeping her parents updated on the investigation and giving them a timeline of when they can claim her remains. As soon as we get what we need here, I'll have them contact you about packing up her things. Thanks for your help. I'll let you know when we're finished." Nicholas took the offered key from the super and closed the door as the older man disappeared into the hallway.

Aubrey swallowed through the tightness in her throat as she studied the bright colors of Paige's bedroom directly on the left, the photos of the victim and her friends and family smiling back from their positions on her dresser. "I hadn't thought about what happens after you close this case. I haven't really had time, I guess. I'll need to make Kara's arrangements after Dr. Caldwell issues the death certificate. My parents will want a funeral, but I'll be the one having to deal with all the details and packing up her apartment. I'll be the one who has to explain to them why she was targeted."

Nicholas's boots echoed off the hardwood as he maneuvered around the end of Paige's bed, those green-blue eyes taking in every detail. A large cutout revealed a straight shot view into the main living space. The double sliding glass door leading out to the third-floor balcony was the only source of natural light in the one-bedroom, one-bathroom apartment, and highlighted the damaged skin along the right side of his face. He raised his gaze to hers. "You think they'll blame you."

"Yes." She hadn't realized how deep that fear had tunneled into the base of her core being. "And why shouldn't they? I do. I'm the end result, aren't I? His masterpiece. He used Kara to get to me, to draw me into this sick mind game, and she was the one who ended up paying the price. How am I supposed to live with that? How am I supposed to face my parents when this case is closed?"

"The same way you've faced everything else

up until now." Nicholas stilled, every ounce of his focus on her, and a massive flood of appreciation filled her.

"With burned doughnuts, cartoons and my very own charming profiler to unload my emotional baggage onto?" Her attempt at a smile failed as her bottom lip trembled. He wasn't just a profiler. Not to her. Over the course of the past four days, he'd become so much more. Her friend, her partner, her anchor in a storm she hadn't seen coming, and a small part of her believed whatever was happening between them could survive this case. That what they'd been through together in that slaughterhouse had forged the invisible connection between them into something stronger. Something unbreakable.

"Don't discount the effects a nice hot shower can have on your mental and physical health, too, Doc." He hit her with a crooked smile, and her gut coiled tighter. "You think I'm charming?"

"Well, you haven't turned and run screaming after finding out what I do for a living, so you've got that going for you." Aubrey picked up the nearest photo the victim had set on top of her dresser near an open jewelry box. Paige's straight, white teeth flashed in a wide smile as she stared up at the man beside her. A boyfriend? From the position of the camera and the height of the victim, it looked as though the man stood at least six inches taller than Paige, putting him around six feet. Dark brown eyes glittered as he pulled Paige into an overexaggerated kiss, bending her backward with the support of both of his hands, and an instant ping resonated behind Aubrey's sternum. Paige had been happy in the photo. In love.

A brilliant diamond ring caught the light from the victim's hand, and she made a visual inspection of the jewelry box beside where the photo had stood. It wasn't there. Scanning the nightstands on either side of the bed, she found them bare. "If we want to find out where the book club met, we'll want to question Paige's fiancé. He might know when and where the meetings occurred."

Nicholas circled around the end of the bed, and she handed him the frame. His hand brushed against her own, resurrecting the delicious tendril of heat she couldn't seem to shake when he was near, and Aubrey wanted nothing more than to hold on to that a bit longer. "Her friends and family never mentioned anything about a fiancé or a boyfriend."

"This photo says otherwise. Paige wouldn't have kept a picture like this unless she was still seeing him, but that's not why I wanted you to look at it. Look at the ring." She pointed to the glistening diamond. "It's not in her jewelry box, and she wasn't wearing an engagement ring when we found her remains on the pier. Dr. Caldwell or his assistant would've noted it in the autopsy report. Medical examiners are required to account for every personal effect taken off the deceased, including cash, jewelry and phones. We have to call it out to our assistants and anyone else around so we can't be accused of stealing from the dead."

"I recognize this guy. I talked to him. He was outside Kara's apartment, behind the perimeter tape." The lines between Nicholas's eyebrows deepened. He turned the photo toward her as though he expected her to remember anything more than discovering her sister's body at that scene. "He told me he was training to become a crime scene photographer. Simon something. Simon… Curry. Said he'd been following my career since the X Marks the Spot case…then he asked about you."

A shiver solidified in her gut. She stared at the photo, willing her brain to take the memories of her attacker and fit them into this mystery man's profile, but she couldn't. Not without hearing his voice. Because no matter how many times she'd tried to bury that sound in a box at the back of her mind, it'd been permanently engraved. She'd never forget that voice, and she never wanted to hear it again. Pieces of conversation broke free from memories of the slaughterhouse.

"The killer said he'd loved Paige, that he was the only one who really knew her." She forced herself to keep her pulse even. She studied the redheaded, muscular man in the photo. Was Simon Curry the killer? "He knew the first victim intimately and was photographing the crime scene of the second. According to Dr. Caldwell, Paige was already dead by the time I discovered Kara outside her apartment, but Simon Curry didn't mention anything about his fiancée being missing?"

"No, and he wasn't the one who reported her missing, either. Her mother called the police after Paige failed to show up for her parents' anniversary party." Nicholas pried the photo from the frame and slid it into his back pocket. Circling back around the queen-size bed, he searched the opening leading into what Aubrey assumed was the victim's closet. "There's no evidence Curry was living here with his fiancée. No clothes hanging in the closet. No men's shoes or any toiletries in the bathroom. If Simon Curry and Paige Cress were engaged, they were keeping it from her family."

"They looked so happy in that photo. Why keep the news to themselves?" she asked.

"I'm not sure yet, but that will be one of the

first questions I ask him when we bring him in for questioning." Nicholas stepped back out into the hallway, the same dead expression she'd noted in her sister's apartment smoothing his rugged features. He maneuvered into the main living space. His boots skimmed across the hardwood floor and seemed overly loud in her ears.

"Paige Cress worked a lot of long nights being one of the most requested paralegals in her firm, which explains the lack of a pet, decor and personalization other than the bedroom. This wasn't a sanctuary to her as Kara's apartment had been. This place was a necessity. Somewhere close to the office where she could sleep and shower then start fresh the next day." He moved into the kitchen lining one wall and opened the refrigerator. "Empty. Her work was her life. She loved her job. She was good at it. Her friends said they hadn't seen her in months because of her busy schedule. So how did she find the time for a serious relationship?"

Aubrey followed on his heels into the living room. Pulling one of the true crime titles they'd identified from the photos taken by Nicholas's team from the bookcase, she opened the hardcover wide. A note in strong, masculine handwriting cut through the book's title page. "'To Paige, my Gingerbread Woman. Never stop searching for the truth. Love, Simon, the Watcher.'"

"The Watcher." Nicholas's voice dipped into dangerous territory as he took the book from her. "That can't be right. Ellis Hull has been behind bars for over a year after being tied to the deaths of twelve tourists, and our victim wasn't the Gingerbread Woman. Evidence proved Irene Lawrence suffocated those women in her law firm after she felt threatened they'd get in the way of her making partner."

"'My Gingerbread Woman.' It's his nickname for her." A flood of warmth raced up her neck. "Simon gave the victim this book. He meant it as an intimate gift. You said Paige's social life had taken a hit with so many hours put in at the office the past few months. Makes sense she most likely met Simon Curry in one of the places she frequents the most, and the connection between Kara and Paige is a true crime book club."

"Simon Curry is a member, too. He's signed his name as the Watcher for Paige." Nicholas studied the left-to-right slanted handwriting in pitch-black ink. "His nickname for her matches the MO by which she was killed."

"It sounds like Paige and Simon used those nicknames for each other." Aubrey pulled the fourth title, *Eat the Darkness: Exposing the Watcher*, from the shelf and read the back summary to herself. "According to this, the Watcher abducted tourists from public areas overseas without anyone noticing. Within a few months, police uncovered their bodies dismembered in a seaside cave. Twelve in total, but the Watcher was apprehended by Interpol within a few months."

She flipped through the book, noting highlights and notes written in feminine handwriting. "It's possible each member of the club took on a nickname inspired by one of the killers they were studying."

"Only Simon took it a step further." Nicholas closed the book, his eyes darker than a few minutes ago. "Claiming a killer's nickname wasn't enough. He was inspired by the real thing."

Chapter Twelve

"I've never been in an interrogation room before. What's the special occasion, Agent James?"

Simon Curry took his seat across the table as Nicholas planted the case file in front of him. Dark eyes, nearly black, scanned the two-tone gray walls, the reinforced electrical outlet to Curry's right and the one-way glass that protected Aubrey from facing a possible suspect in her abduction on the other side. A thick red beard failed to hide the slight nervousness of the man's mouth. Curry's forehead wrinkles deepened as Nicholas sat across the stainless-steel table. At six feet, Simon Curry matched the musculature and height of the bastard who'd attacked him and Aubrey at the pier, but it would take a lot more than the suspect's frame to tie him to two murders. "Does the BAU need the photos I took at the crime scene the other day?"

"No, Simon. The photographer we have on staff did a great job. We have everything we need from the scene." Nicholas opened the file in front of him and pulled a stack of developed and oversize photos from Kara Flood's crime scene free, including those documenting the victim outside her apartment. Positioning them one next to the other across the table, Nicholas watched Simon's expression bleed from excitement to disbelief. "Do you recognize this woman?"

"That's X Marks... That's Kara." Simon pushed the photos back across the table as a tendril of anger surfaced. "She was the victim at the crime scene? Holy hell, why are you showing these to me?"

"You were going to call her X Marks the Spot, weren't you?" Nicholas asked. "The nickname she took on as a member of the same true crime book club you're part of."

Curry crossed his arms over his chest—defensive—and avoided looking at the crime scene photos in front of him. He raised one hand in a dismissive gesture, and hints of the man's aftershave filled the space between Nicholas and the suspect.

"I'm part of a book club. So what? We all take on the nickname we're assigned during our first meeting. It's tradition, and Kara... She was always so interested in the X Marks the Spot Killer case because her sister was the medical examiner assigned to the investigation. She kept asking questions, seeing if anyone knew something more than what was in the book we were reading, and the name just kind of stuck with her. She thought it would give her something to talk about with her sister, that learning about the case would bring them closer. She would always brag about how Dr. Flood was the one who gave the BAU what they needed to identify Cole Presley. She was proud of her."

Nicholas glanced toward the one-way glass, easily envisioning Aubrey on the other side. Kara Flood had joined the true crime book club to understand her sister, to show she cared about her, to show she loved her. With all the friends and family who'd turned their backs on Aubrey because of her work as a medical examiner, Kara had been in the process of showing her sister how proud she was of her before she'd died. "And what about Paige Cress?"

Three distinct lines appeared between Curry's eyebrows. "What about her?"

"Paige was a member of the book club, too, right? And you and she were involved intimately? Although Paige's family and friends don't recall her having a boyfriend or a fiancé." He unpocketed the photo he and Aubrey had discovered in the victim's apartment and unfolded it before sliding it across the table.

"Where did you get this?" Simon asked.

"Paige's apartment. This, too." He tugged the book Aubrey had taken from the victim's bookcase and opened it to the title page. "This is your handwriting, right? Paige called you her Watcher and you called her your Gingerbread Woman."

"Why do you have this? Why do you have any of this?" Simon's voice echoed off the bare walls as he picked up the photo of him and the first victim. "What's going on here?"

"Paige Cress is dead, Simon, but I have the feeling you already knew that." Nicholas tugged another set of crime scene photos from the case file and spread them over the top of the first. "She was murdered and dumped in a maintenance shed at the waterfront up to twenty hours before you showed up at Kara Flood's crime scene. Suffocated. Just like the Gingerbread Woman suffocated her victims. I'm sure you know the case, considering your true crime book club read the book detailing the investigation recently. Paige was a paralegal, she was suffocated with her own jacket and a photo of her body was found at Kara Flood's crime scene. It all lines up."

"No. This…this isn't happening. Paige can't be dead." Simon pushed away from the table, his chair hitting the back wall, and every muscle in Nicholas's body hardened with battle-ready tension. Only this time, the son of a bitch wouldn't take him or Aubrey by surprise. In fact, he'd never lay a hand on the medical examiner again.

Curry speared both hands through his hair and fisted chunks. It was all a very good act. The apparent grief, the shock. "It was a stupid fight. She isn't dead."

Nicholas straightened. "What fight?"

"Paige was getting cold feet about the wedding. We hadn't told anybody we were engaged because her family wanted her to focus on her career before she settled down, but I didn't want to lie to them anymore. She didn't want to tell them until we were already married. She wanted to elope, but I tried to talk her out of it. She made me move my stuff out of her apartment that night and told me she needed some time to think about her future, but when I left five days ago, she was still alive. She won't answer my messages or call me back." Curry scrubbed a hand down his face. "And now...are you positive the body you found is her?"

"The county medical examiner confirmed her identity through dental records and a fracture Paige sustained when she was younger. X-rays don't lie." Nicholas gathered the photos back into the case file and closed the manila folder. "I need you to tell me where you were between nine and midnight the night after your fight with Paige, Simon, and I need the contact information of anybody who can corroborate your whereabouts at that time."

"Is that…is that when she… I knew I shouldn't have left her alone. We could've worked it out. Maybe if I hadn't pushed her, she'd still be alive." Confusion overwhelmed the grief in the suspect's expression. Curry regained a small amount of control, his shoulders rising on a strong inhale as he clutched the back of the chair. "That night. I, uh, I went back to my apartment. I spent the rest of the night drinking myself stupid in front of the TV. Alone."

"No one can vouch for you that you were in your apartment all night?" he asked. "What about a bite mark? Paige Cress bit her attacker before she died. Can you prove it wasn't your skin the medical examiner pulled from between her teeth?"

"Paige and I were engaged. We were sleeping together. Sometimes it got more passionate than we planned. She'd bite and scratch me all the time, but that doesn't mean I killed her." Anger strengthened the level of Simon Curry's voice again. "You said Paige was murdered with the same MO the Gingerbread Woman used on her victims, and from the photos you showed me of Kara Flood, she was killed with the X Marks the Spot Killer's MO. Strangled with an *X* carved into her right cheek. Both of them were killed with the same MO as their nicknames, so it had to be someone from the book club."

"I'm going to need a list of members, Simon," Nicholas said.

"I don't have a list. We don't… We don't know each other's real names or see each other outside the club. We call each other by our nicknames," Curry said. "We just met at some after-hours coffee shop called AfterDark."

"You and Paige shared your real names. You had a relationship outside the club. You were living together. The proof is right there on the title page of this book you gifted her." Nicholas wrote down the name of the coffee shop in his notepad and motioned to the book in front of him. "And you recognized Kara Flood."

"Paige and I were an anomaly. We didn't mean for it to happen. It just…did. I loved her. I was ready to spend the rest of my life with her." Curry enunciated his point with an index finger pressed into the surface of the table between them. "And Kara let her real name slip during a discussion a few months back. She wanted us to know she was related to the medical examiner who worked the X Marks the Spot Killer case, and Paige took advantage of it. They started a true crime podcast together. It was really taking off, bringing in a lot of sponsorship opportunities."

"Kara told the book club Dr. Aubrey Flood was her sister, then she and Paige went into business together?" That must've been how Kara Flood had been able to afford her apartment in that neighborhood, but she'd never told Aubrey, and the BAU hadn't found any evidence of recording equipment in either of their apartments. A coil of unwanted protectiveness twisted in Nicholas's gut.

Aubrey wasn't the only one who was afraid to close her eyes after what'd happened in that slaughterhouse, but he'd managed to get through his past cases alone. He'd do it again. "Funny you should mention Dr. Flood, because the same day we discovered your fiancée's body on that pier, someone about your height and weight attacked Aubrey Flood. Hung her upside down by her ankles in a slaughterhouse and nicked her carotid artery to make her bleed out." The anger Nicholas had struggled to contain before he'd stepped inside this room with Simon Curry flared. "That takes medical training, and it turns out you dropped out of medical school last year in pursuit of becoming a crime scene photographer. You see this photo?"

He extracted the Polaroid of Paige Cress's remains that'd been recovered in the back of the cargo van near Kara Flood's death scene with her dog inside.

"The killer left this picture of Paige at the crime scene where you were spotted hugging the perimeter tape with your camera. You had knowledge of that case, and you're good with a camera. The killer lured my team to the pier so we could recover her remains, knowing Dr. Flood would be invested in finding out the connection between Paige and her sister. You admitted yourself you were fascinated with Dr. Flood and her work on the X Killer case. The killer also used a scalpel to nick Dr. Flood's carotid artery with a steady hand. You have a medical background."

Nicholas pressed his elbows in the table and leaned forward, his gaze locked on Simon Curry. "I think you lured us there to get Aubrey Flood all to yourself, Simon. I think you've read so many books about serial killers, you've convinced yourself you're capable of outshining them all, but you needed practice first. So you killed Paige, and when that didn't give you the satisfaction you craved, you moved on to Kara Flood to complicate the game and draw her sister closer. It's the love of the chase, isn't it? That's what you crave. You want to prove you're better than the killers you've idolized all these years. You want to prove you're better than me and my team, but that's not how this is going to end, Simon. You're not better. You're just a copycat."

Simon pried his hands from the back of the chair and calmly took his seat across from Nicholas. He interlaced his fingers on the surface of the table and dropped his chin, severing eye contact. "I'm not saying another word without my lawyer."

THEY HAD HIM. Simon Curry had the means, the motive and the opportunity, not to mention a connection to both victims, but doubt curdled in her stomach. It was the voice. That wasn't the voice of the man who'd abducted and tried to kill her. She was sure of it.

Aubrey studied the suspect on the other side of the glass before the door to the observation room swung open. Goose pimples climbed her arms and puckered across her back as Nicholas settled that intelligent gaze on her. "All the evidence seems to line up against him, and he has no alibi."

"But you aren't convinced he's the one who attacked you." Not a question. He didn't need to ask. Nicholas seemed to see right through her, understand her, and the unexpected connection between them vibrated stronger. He faced the one-way glass, his reflection highlighting the stitches and deformities along the curve of his jaw, but the damage hadn't lessened her attraction. Nothing could. "He has a medical background, a connection to both victims and the knowledge base of how serials work. Hell, he even admitted his admiration for you."

It all made sense. She couldn't argue with that, and the people pleaser she'd allowed herself to become over the course of her life screamed at her to sit down and avoid rocking the boat. But she wasn't that woman anymore, and she wouldn't help put Simon Curry behind bars unless she was absolutely positive he'd been the one behind that ski mask. It would be easy to agree with Nicholas and the BAU about the man in the interrogation room, but she couldn't. "It's not him."

Nicholas shifted his weight between both feet, and the tension in the room notched higher. Lowering his gaze along the edge of the bottom of the large window, he turned his head slightly toward her, disappointment clear in his expression. "You've been through a lot over the past few days, Aubrey. Trauma alters memories of things we're positive happened or that we heard. It's possible you're misremembering details of your attack or you're afraid of confronting those memories fully in order to protect yourself."

He didn't believe her.

"You think I don't want it to be Simon Curry? That I want the man who did this to me to go free?" But worse than that, that she wasn't strong enough to face what'd happened to her? Uninhibited betrayal exploded through her as she stepped away from the window. "I've been at your side every step of the way on this case, Nicholas. I almost died trying to help you find the killer who murdered my sister, and now you're telling me I can't be a reliable source because of what I went through? I remember what he sounds like *because* of what I went through."

His expression remained cool, under control, when everything inside her wanted to scream and rail, and suddenly this wasn't the man who'd attempted to make her doughnuts, who'd held her while watching her favorite cartoon. Who'd kissed her and helped her realize she needed to put her needs first for once. "It's not me, Doc. Claiming that's not the guy who attacked you on the pier based off his voice isn't evidence, and it won't hold up in court. You know that."

Nicholas faced her, something along the lines of regret pulling the tendons between his neck and shoulders tight. "You went to medical school. You've seen the research. You've read the studies proving trauma affects people differently, and you have to admit the only reason you kissed me is because you needed someone to help you get through it."

His words registered as though he'd physically thrown a blow, and she backed up until her thighs hit the edge of a table positioned a few feet away for balance. Disbelief gripped her heart in a vise. Was that what he really believed? That she'd used him for her own selfishness and coping? What kind of person did he think she was? "That's not...that's not why I kissed you. You think that's why I kissed you?"

"All I'm saying is your memories of what happened might not be accurate, Doc. Simon Curry fits the profile, and he doesn't have anyone to corroborate his whereabouts when Paige Cress or your sister were killed," he said. "Do you want a jury to find him innocent after your testimony because one detail feels off to you?"

His blow struck again, harder, and if she hadn't been braced against the table, Aubrey feared she might've crumpled right there in the middle of the floor. Her heart jackhammered in her chest, pounding so wildly that the cracks around the edges started to shatter. She'd requested Nicholas James to solve her sister's case, but she'd stupidly taken his affection and promises to heart. She'd imagined them closing this investigation and moving on to the next. Imagined waking up to the smell of burned doughnuts and hearing the voices of her favorite cartoon each morning before they left for their respective jobs. Imagined them trying to top one another with funny sayings and laughing, committed. Together. Happy. She deserved to be happy. Why was he doing this?

Aubrey forced herself to stand a bit straighter, to retreat behind the barrier she'd built from having one more person take advantage of her. He wasn't going to be the one to walk away this time. Anger bled into her voice. "I remember everything that happened after I pulled you from the ocean, Agent James. Every second, every minute. I remember the pain as he knocked me unconscious with a wrench. I remember the pressure in my head and chest when I realized he'd hung me by my ankles. I remember what he smelled like, his voice in my ear and the way his gloves warmed against my neck before he cut my throat. I remember the agony I sustained after I hit the cement so I could make sure you were alive."

She pushed away from the table, closing the space between them. She slid her hand into his jacket pocket and extracted his SUV's keys. "And when you and I were in that safe house, I remember how good it felt for someone to put me first for once, and how I'd finally found someone I didn't have to hide myself from. Someone who I could imagine being happy with, but maybe you're right. Maybe I can't rely on my memories after all."

Aubrey headed for the door and swung it wide,

stepping out into the hall. She secured the door behind her but didn't have the strength to release her grip from the knob as everything she'd recounted came into question. The evidence pointed to Simon Curry as her sister's killer, but she wouldn't be able to walk into a courtroom to testify unless she was sure.

There was only one way to prove he hadn't murdered Kara.

She had to see her sister's remains for herself.

Prying her fingers from around the observation room door handle, she wound her way through the FBI's Seattle office and out into the floor's lobby. Two bays of elevators pinged, and she waited for one of the cars to clear before stepping on, tears burning in her eyes.

The doors started to slide closed, promising escape, before a hand slipped through and triggered the automatic sensor. "Hold it!"

A familiar smile flashed back at her, and Aubrey moved aside to allow the passenger room. She almost hadn't recognized him without his lab coat and face shield, but the long, straight nose, thick eyebrows, and smallish eyes punctured through the haze of spiraling hurt. Graying temples emphasized his elongated facial structure, but his five-o'clock shadow instantly set her at ease. She smoothed her uninjured hand down her slacks. "Dr. Caldwell, I didn't expect to see you here. I imagine the FBI's case is keeping you quite busy."

"Dr. Flood, how good to see you. Yes, it's been quite the experience working this investigation with the BAU. Now I know why you've been keeping them all to yourself." His rich laugh hitched as the elevator descended from the penthouse. "I'd heard you'd been attacked. I'm so sorry. I didn't realize the extent of your injuries. May I ask the diagnosis?"

"Fractured scapula along with two of my right sternal ribs. It'll be a few months of recovery, but I'm managing. I should be able to return to work soon." The lie fell from her mouth easily enough, but she wasn't about to break down in front of a colleague, and sure as hell not in this building. Her gaze flickered to the security camera in the corner of the elevator car. No. She wouldn't give Nicholas the satisfaction of seeing her cry. Denial charged up her throat as Nicholas's accusation filtered through the county medical examiner's concerned expression.

"Always the optimist. That's one of the things I like about you. If anyone could force a fracture to heal quickly, it'd be you." Dr. Caldwell's voice lowered an octave, and the walls seemed to close in around her. "You always were the best. I imagine that's why the FBI chose you to work the X Marks the Spot Killer case over me three years ago."

"In perspective of experience and years dedicated to your work, Dr. Caldwell, you are obviously the choice the FBI should've made for that case. It was simply being available when the case agent needed a pathologist at the time. I believe you were tied up with another homicide investigation when Agent James invited me to investigate the case." His hint of jealousy spiked through her, and Aubrey forced herself to stare straight ahead at her reflection in the steel doors, but the weight of being watched pressurized the air in her lungs. She cleared her throat. "I was actually headed to your office. The BAU has a suspect in custody—Simon Curry. He had the means and opportunity to target both victims without a confirmed alibi, but I'm not convinced he's responsible. I'd like to take a look at my sister's remains, if that's possible. See if there is something that can tie Simon Curry directly to both murders."

"You think I missed something during the autopsy?" he asked.

"No. Not at all, Dr. Caldwell. I'd simply like to see Kara for myself. Call it a personal favor. I'd owe you." The elevator jostled as it descended to the parking level, and she clutched the keys she'd taken from Nicholas hard enough to bite the skin of her palm. The doors opened, and a wall of humidity settled against her face and neck. Relief coursed through her veins as she stepped off the elevator and added another few hundred feet between her and the profiler upstairs. She called back over her shoulder. "We could drive together, if you prefer."

No response.

Aubrey slowed her escape and looked back. The elevator doors remained open, exposing the empty car within. She searched the parking garage, but there wasn't any sign of him. The nearest vehicle was still a few feet ahead of her. He wouldn't have been able to reach his own car that quickly. She'd just have to meet Dr. Caldwell at his own office. Forcing one step in front of the other, she kept herself together long enough to reach Nicholas's SUV, but the tears were already breaking through. She hit the button to unlock the driver's-side door.

She'd spent most of her life feeling alone, unwanted. She'd get through this.

Pain exploded across the back of her head as she reached for the SUV's door handle, and she slammed up against the window. Inky blackness spidered across her vision as Aubrey battled to face her attacker, but it was no use. She was slipping to the ground and into unconsciousness.

Chapter Thirteen

He hadn't seen the threat coming.

Nicholas tossed the case file onto his desk and slumped into his seat. Aubrey Flood had walked into his life and taken out his defenses with a sweet smile and an underhanded charm. And hell, he hated himself for it. He hated that he could be manipulated so easily, that he hadn't been able to protect himself against her warmth and patience before it was too late. Cole Presley had done the same thing. The bastard had used Nicholas's own trust against him then shattered his world when the truth surfaced. The X Marks the Spot Killer had worn a human mask to hide the monster underneath. How was he supposed to trust Aubrey hadn't done the same, that her mask wasn't as much of a lie as Cole's had been? How was he supposed to know if the vulnerable, intelligent, beautiful woman he'd grown closer to over this investigation was real?

His cell vibrated from his slacks pocket, and

he pulled the device free, answering in the same move. "Tell me you were able to confirm After-Dark is the location the book club met and find a barista or a customer who can give a description of all the members."

"Yes and no," David Dyson said. "For a coffee shop, AfterDark prides itself on ensuring their customers' privacy. Neither the owner nor any of the baristas would talk to me, and they don't have any cameras. But I was able to match purchases from both victims' financials to purchases made at this location. I'm waiting outside to catch a couple customers as they leave. See if I can't get something more from some of the regulars."

"Good work, Dyson." Nicholas leaned back in his chair. "Let me know what you find."

He disconnected the call. The evidence pointed to Simon Curry as the killer, but damn it, Aubrey's confidence they'd brought in the wrong man tunneled through logic and straight past rationale. He believed her. It'd been in her voice. In the way she'd studied the suspect and held her ground. Any other victim would've collapsed after facing the possibility of being within arm's reach of the person who'd tortured them, but not her. She'd gone against his every instinct and demanded he see things her way instead of bowing down to the inner people pleaser she'd sacrificed herself for, and hell, he admired her for it.

Loved her for it.

"Well, call me a purple hippo." Nicholas ran both hands through his hair. He loved her. He wasn't sure when it'd happened, wasn't sure he cared, but he'd fallen for the medical examiner he hadn't been able to forget for the past three years. He'd been an idiot. Of course he'd fallen for her. Despite the fact she used to make her sister play pretend homicide victim as kids and her taste buds had stopped working, as evidenced by her eating the doughnuts he'd made her, Aubrey was the most generous, driven and unselfish woman he'd known. She'd gone out of her way to put others first, to the point of losing herself in the process, and he couldn't hold her newfound confidence against her.

If anything, her defiance to comply with his suspicion against Simon Curry only made him love her more. She'd stood up for herself, and damn, that fire in her gaze had been one of the sexiest things he'd ever seen. Until he'd doused it by using her mental trauma after her attack against her. Nicholas set his elbows on his desk, staring at the case file without really seeing anything clearly. "You sure are a son of a bitch."

He'd taken his own fear of trusting again and weaponized it against the one woman who'd calmed the uncertainty he'd carried all these years. It'd been easy to discount her claim of

Simon Curry's innocence, especially given the evidence seemed to line up against Paige Cress's fiancé, but Nicholas had never felt more wrong in his life. The past three days had shown him a life he hadn't imagined for himself. Aubrey had single-handedly broken through the doubt he'd held on to since discovering who Cole Presley really was that day. She'd looked at him as though he were the most capable, most intelligent and innovative BAU agent, to the point he'd started believing her. She'd done that. She'd given him the confidence and forced him to look at his positive qualities rather than focusing on his failures, and he'd thrown that service in her face.

He had to find her. He had to make this right.

The atmosphere in the office ratcheted higher. A swarm of agents jogged to the other side of the building. Nicholas rounded his desk, leaving his office, and spotted SSA Miguel Peters shouting orders from behind the conference room glass. Something had happened. He could feel it.

Nicholas caught sight of Dashiell West circling around the doors and wound his way through the maze of agents. He pushed through the wall of the FBI's finest, threaded his hand around West's arm and spun the cybercrimes agent toward him. "West, what's going on?"

"There's been an attack in the parking garage." Color drained from the cybercrimes agent's face, and dread pooled at the base of Nicholas's spine. The surrounding agents stilled, the weight of their attention burrowing deep in his chest. "Security reported the camera in one of the elevators had been disabled. I went through the footage leading up to the blackout and discovered the surveillance in the garage had also been shut down. They've swept the garage, but the only evidence they were able to uncover was a book near your SUV."

Air caught in his chest. "What book?"

"*But First, Lipstick*, the true crime book detailing the Extreme Makeover Killer's investigation." West seemed to prepare himself as though Nicholas would attack at the news that came next. "There was only one other person who got on the elevator with her, Nicholas, and we can't locate or get in touch with him, either. It was Dr. Caldwell."

Son of a bitch. Aubrey had been right. He replayed the interactions between him and the killer. The bastard's size, medical knowledge, his obsession with Aubrey. Hell, narcissistic behavior was common among medical professionals because of their overwhelming God complex of having lives in their hands. His background as an army combat medic, medical school and years on the job accredited the pathologist with enough experience around a scalpel, and the jealousy West had picked up on was more than enough motive to put Aubrey at the center of the killer's sick game. Simon Curry might've had the means, motive, opportunity and connections to kill Kara Flood and Paige Cress, but so had the King County medical examiner. Dr. Archer Caldwell was a member of the same true crime book club both victims had met with, and his jealousy of Aubrey being invited to work the X Marks the Spot investigation had pushed him to the edge. With Simon Curry in custody, it was the only explanation. Dr. Caldwell had claimed the Extreme Makeover Killer's nickname and left the book as a taunt. The parking garage. Nicholas released his grip on West. "Give me your keys."

"We don't have a location yet." West handed them over, and Nicholas raced toward the stairs. The agent's voice barely registered through the pounding of Nicholas's heart behind his ears. "How are you going to find her?"

"He's headed to the underground!" Nicholas had never been so sure of anything in his life. It fit the Extreme Makeover Killer's MO. Caldwell would see Aubrey's survival from the events at the slaughterhouse as a personal failure, possibly grounds to remove Aubrey as the one he'd chosen as his own masterpiece. If that was the case as Nicholas believed, the pathologist would retreat back to an MO he was familiar with, one he'd studied before moving on to look for another prize. One guaranteed to kill his victim. Samson Little had bound his victims before cutting their wrists and watching them slowly bleed out, but he hadn't wanted them discovered. Just as he hadn't wanted his wife discovered, but the dead always found a way to speak. Aubrey had taught him that.

Nicholas pushed into the stairwell and sprinted down the stairs. The snap of the door slamming into the wall behind it exploded like a gunshot above, and he looked up long enough to recognize Agents Striker and West and SSA Peters following close behind. They had a location. They were going to find her alive. There wasn't another option. Not for him.

Stale air slammed into him as Nicholas ripped open the garage-level door. Targeting his SUV and the security team sweeping the area around it, he called to the security lead as his team spread across the garage from behind. "Any progress?"

"No, sir. Not yet," the team lead said. "I'll report all findings to you as soon as we have something. We're doing a sweep for Dr. Caldwell's vehicle now and have contacted Seattle PD."

Nicholas ran for West's SUV as Striker and the cybercrimes agent loaded into hers. SSA Peters climbed into the passenger seat as Nicholas climbed behind the wheel. He twisted the key in the ignition and ripped out of the parking garage. Sunlight pierced through the windshield as he fishtailed onto Union toward Second Avenue and Pioneer Square. "He's headed for the Seattle underground. He's going to use Aubrey to re-create the Extreme Makeover's MO and leave her there for us to search blocks of underground to find her."

"This guy hasn't stuck to any one MO since he started. There could be a thousand locations within the city alone he's taken her if you're wrong about this." SSA Peters braced against the passenger-side door as Nicholas took the left onto Second above the speed limit. "What makes you so sure she'll be underground?"

"The book Dr. Caldwell left behind. Both victims were members of the same true crime book club, and one of the books on their shelves was *But First, Lipstick*, which gives an account of the Extreme Makeover Killer. According to Simon Curry, every member in the club took on a nickname of their favorite serial killer. Kara Flood was invested in learning about the X Marks the Spot Killer because Aubrey had been involved in the case. Paige Cress was the Gingerbread Woman, and Simon Curry claimed the Watcher."

If he hadn't pushed to put Curry in the dark silhouette of their perp on the murder board, he might've seen it before. There weren't more victims out there they hadn't discovered. Not yet. "Caldwell had to have been in the same book club. He would've known their nicknames. He replicated his idols' MOs to test his skills before he turned his attention to his real target."

"Dr. Flood," SSA Peters said.

"Aubrey isn't a member. I think he got tired of Kara talking about her sister during the meetings. He's jealous of her. He wants to make an example of her, to prove he's the better pathologist and that he should've been the one to handle the X Killer case. He's punishing her." Nicholas tightened his grip around the steering wheel, and he pushed the SUV harder. "He left the book for me. He wanted me to know his nickname was the Extreme Makeover Killer and that that was exactly how he was going to murder Aubrey once his own MO failed to kill her."

"It's public knowledge the Extreme Makeover Killer dumped all his victims' bodies in the underground. Why make the game so easy?" SSA Peters asked. "Why follow an MO to a tee when police already have the location of the dump site?"

"Because he thinks he can get away with it." The ego and arrogance had been right in front of him all this time. This wasn't about the manner Dr. Caldwell had chosen or with which he'd killed his victims. They'd been nothing but a convenience of which he'd taken advantage. Every move, every lead the BAU had taken uncovered nothing but pure narcissism.

"He craves the chase, and he's worked for the county as a medical examiner long enough to ensure none of the forensic evidence ties back to him. He's been involved in the investigation. He's had access to the remains of his two victims. He knows everything we had aside from the piece of tissue Paige Cress had between her teeth was circumstantial, and he's probably already destroyed it. This is one big game to him, and he took her because I let my own trust issues get in the way of protecting her."

And he feared Aubrey wouldn't be the last victim to pay the price if he failed.

HUMMING FILLED HER EARS.

There was no pressure this time. No crushing pain other than the constant ache in her ribs as she filled her lungs with cold, dry air, and the pounding at the back of her skull where her attacker had hit her. She wasn't upside down. Aubrey hauled her chin away from her chest, an old wooden chair protesting as she moved. The torn skin of her left wrist burned under the friction of rope securing her to the chair.

"Ah, Dr. Flood. Nice to see you again." Dr.

Caldwell's outline darkened the spotlight shining into her face. He bent at the waist, coming that much closer to the point she caught hints of formaldehyde and cleaning agent. "While you were unconscious, I gained access to your recent X-rays after our first little meeting. Thank you for telling the truth about your diagnosis. Your fractured scapula and broken ribs, coupled with a change in binds, gives me confidence you won't be able to struggle this time."

She swept her tongue through her mouth to chase back the dryness and taste of dirt. The edges of the gauze on her neck pulled at her over-sensitized skin. Mustiness embedded into her lung tissue as she rolled her head to one side. An exposed brick arch and cement flooring materialized as her eyes adjusted to the overstimulation from the spotlight. Strong pillars had cracked under the pressure of the slight bulge in the ceiling, and Aubrey felt as though she were deep underground. Far enough no one could hear her scream. "Dr. Caldwell—Archer—what...what are you doing?"

"I'm proving I'm better, of course." The voice that'd been stuck in her head since the attack grated against every fiber of her being, but she hadn't recognized Dr. Caldwell for the killer he was. The only explanation she had was his voice wasn't altered by a ski mask now. "You, of all people, should understand that, Dr. Flood. You've gone out of your way to become the FBI's favorite pathologist these past few years. Well, now I'm going out of my way to prove I was the better choice." Dr. Caldwell turned slightly, the spotlight highlighting the sharp angles of his face and illuminating a cruel smile. "And believe me, after I'm finished with you, they'll never doubt my abilities again."

Disbelief hardened the muscles along her spine. That was what this was about? Her sister had been strangled and mutilated because he hadn't been chosen to work the X Marks the Spot Killer case? "You were in the same book club as Kara and Paige, weren't you? You used their nicknames to replicate previous serial MOs, to show the FBI you were better at killing than the originals, and set up Simon Curry to take the fall."

"Everything would've gone according to plan if Paige Cress hadn't bit me while I was trying to suffocate her with her own jacket, but as the official pathologist over this case, all I had to do was compromise the skin sample my assistant discovered during the initial examination. The lab will never be able to trace the DNA in that skin sample recovered from Paige back to me or connect me to Kara. Everything the FBI has right now is circumstantial." Dr. Caldwell smirked, and Aubrey pulled at the restraints around both feet and her left wrist. "But you... You had to go and be your own hero in the slaughterhouse. You had to attract the affection of Agent James and bring the whole BAU team to my door."

Nicholas. Her insides hollowed as the last few minutes of their conversation in the observation room hit her all over again. She'd been right about Simon Curry. The true killer had methodically made Curry the FBI's prime suspect while working under their noses from the beginning. Dr. Caldwell wasn't just intelligent, as Nicholas had suggested in his profile. He was a genius, and right then Aubrey couldn't see a way of escape.

She followed the exposed pipes above to the end of a long corridor. The headache at the back of her skull intensified the harder she tried to map an escape route, and she rolled her injured shoulder back to test her rotation. Her right hand was the only extremity that hadn't been bound to the chair, still useless in the sling. If she could distract Dr. Caldwell long enough and work through the pain, she might have a chance. "You used Kara to get to me."

"Would you believe me if I told you I'd joined the book club for the same reason as your sister?" His voice hitched as though paired with a smile, and her gut soured. "Kara was all too happy to regale me with stories of her big sister, the medical examiner who'd single-handedly taken down the X Marks the Spot Killer by narrowing down the kind of knife Cole Presley had used to carve his victims' cheeks. That was why she became a member of our little group. She wasn't sure how to talk to you about the investigation face-to-face, so she learned everything she could about the case in order to feel closer to you. A waste of time. Why study the pathologist assigned to the case when she could learn so much more from a killer?"

Kara had been trying to learn as much as she could about the X Marks the Spot Killer case in order to be closer to Aubrey. Simon Curry had said as much during his interrogation, but it wasn't until this moment she was able to process the information in the wake of losing her connection to Nicholas. Her body hurt, but it was nothing compared to the pain in her heart. All this time she'd believed Kara had never understood her, never wanted to understand her, but the opposite had been true.

Dragging a chair she hadn't seen until then closer, Dr. Caldwell took a seat across from her, his expression cast into darkness from the spotlight at his back. "Seems everyone just can't get enough of you, Dr. Flood, including your own family. I'll be honest, I don't understand the fascination. Kara's, Agent James's. You're an above-average pathologist from Seattle, dedicated to your work with little social life or hobbies, as far as I can tell. No serious relationships. If I hadn't known Kara was your sister from our conversations during book club or that your parents were still alive, I would've assumed you were utterly and completely alone. That leaves the X Marks the Spot Killer case. If it hadn't been for that investigation—for your connection to such a high-profile case—you'd be nothing."

"Maybe the fact that I'm not a psychopath has something to do with it." She blinked against the white lights developing across her vision from the unrelenting brightness of the spotlight.

"I underestimated you before, Dr. Flood." A low laugh punctuated Dr. Caldwell's rise to his feet. He turned away from her. He disappeared into the shadows fighting to close in around the pool of spotlight, his voice more distant than a minute ago. Shuffling sounds ensued from the darkness, a hit of metal breaking through. Another scalpel? "But I won't make the same mistake twice."

Aubrey secured her jaw against the bone-deep ache in her shoulder and ribs as she pushed her elbow toward the outer edge of her sling. Dr. Caldwell had been assigned to an investigation of his own making. Her heart rate rocketed into overdrive as the pain spread outward from her scapula and nearly pulled a groan from her throat. She forced herself to keep her breathing under control as she worked her injured arm free of the sling. Too much force and the tendons keeping her bone from separating completely would snap, causing irreversible damage. Too little and she'd never get free. The lining of the sling scraped against her heated skin, but she couldn't stop. She'd escaped Dr. Caldwell once before. She could do it again.

Nicholas had believed the killer was driven by his narcissistic personality disorder, desperate to prove himself better than the men and women he idolized. That desperation meant he wouldn't be able to turn down the opportunity to talk about himself. "You disposed of Paige Cress's body on the pier to draw me there. There weren't any signs she'd been killed in that shed. You had to have killed her somewhere else. The evidence on her body might've been compromised, but the scent of gasoline was still on her clothes when we found her. The forensic lab will be able to pick up traces."

A lie. The techs hadn't been able to recover anything after the ocean had washed the victim's clothes, but the Gingerbread Woman had attacked all her victims in parking garages. He'd stuck to every last detail concerning the X Marks the Spot Killer's MO. Made sense he'd do the same for the Gingerbread Woman's. "It was a garage, wasn't it? Agent James and the rest of the BAU will find which one. It's only a matter of time before he ties you to these crimes."

"Your profiler surely believes I'm a narcissist, and you've interpreted that to mean getting me to talk about myself and the way I kill will give you a chance for escape. You're wrong." Dr. Caldwell stepped back into the spotlight, and every cell in her body spiked into awareness. The outline of a blade in his hand, similar to the shape of a No. 11 scalpel used to make fine incisions during an autopsy, demanded attention as he stepped closer. He leaned into her, setting the cold steel against her cheek.

"You're forgetting I was the pathologist assigned to examine the victims, and I ensured none of the evidence the forensic lab tested would trace back to me. Cole Presley, Irene Lawrence, Samson Little—they might've been the inspiration for my masterpieces, but I've risen above them. Even if the BAU arrests me for the deaths of Kara Flood and Paige Cress, they'll never be able to prove it, and you won't live long enough to tell them what happened here today. I'm sorry to disappoint you, Dr. Flood, but I can't be beat."

The steel of the scalpel warmed against her cheek. Aubrey twisted her head sharply and bit down on her attacker's hand as hard as she could. Blood penetrated the seam of her lips and filled her mouth, triggering her gag reflex, but she only clamped her teeth harder. Her attacker's scream echoed off the brick walls, and he tore his hand away. But not fast enough. She forced herself to swallow as he held on to his bleeding hand, and a sense of accomplishment filled her. "Let's see you compromise that sample."

Dr. Caldwell arced the scalpel down toward her wrist bound to the chair and sank it deep through tendon, veins and muscle. Aubrey's scream rivaled her abductor's and intensified the pain in her head, but she couldn't pull away. His hand shook around the blade as he stared down at her. "Let's see how much you bleed."

Chapter Fourteen

"All tourists have been accounted for and evacuated, Agent James." The Seattle PD officer's staticky voice barely registered from the radio strapped to Nicholas's vest.

Pinholes of light penetrated through the street-level grid-pattern glass skywalk above as he and the team descended into history. The network of underground passageways and basements in downtown Pioneer Square had originally been ground level when the city was built in the mid-nineteenth century, but the Seattle Great Fire had relegated a maze of shops and spaces to disuse. With fewer and fewer guided tours through the labyrinth, it'd been the perfect location for the Extreme Makeover Killer to dump his victims' bodies, but Nicholas wasn't going to let Aubrey become the newest resident.

"This guy is intelligent, beyond what we originally estimated, and dangerous. He's planned this out from the beginning, and he won't give

Aubrey up easily. Stay alert, watch each other's backs and keep in radio contact."

"Striker, West, take the left corridor. James, you're with me." SSA Peters unholstered his weapon as they split at the first intersection of passages. "We want Dr. Caldwell alive, but if you have to shoot the bastard to protect yourself or the victim, I won't feel bad about it."

"Copy," Striker said.

"See you on the other side." West laughed, following his partner.

Exposed piping above led them deeper into the man-made caverns, past shattered window fronts and through inches of dust, ash and debris. Nicholas angled his flashlight toward the ground, sweeping it across the broken, aged cement in an effort to pick up some kind of trail. Humidity worked deep into his lungs as he scanned the inside of the old store on his right. No movement. Nothing to suggest Dr. Caldwell or Aubrey had been here at all. His pulse ticked hard at the base of his throat. These tunnels ran the length of five city blocks in some areas and had become basements to galleries, restaurants and tourist traps on the surface. The killer could've taken her anywhere.

A scream resonated down the tunnel.

"Aubrey." She was alive. Nicholas bolted down the corridor in the direction he believed the sound had originated, his flashlight and weapon bouncing in his hand. His legs protested the harder he ran, but nothing would stop him from getting to her this time. The blueprint he'd memorized before they'd descended into the city's underworld stayed fresh in his mind as he came to another break in the maze, and he pulled up short. Two directions. Nicholas searched both passages, but he couldn't see a damn thing, couldn't hear her. If he chose wrong, it'd cost Aubrey more time. It could cost her her life.

Pressure clawed up his throat. He couldn't fail her again. His heart threatened to beat straight out of his chest. "Damn it."

The sound of footsteps fell into line behind him as SSA Peters kept close on his heels. The supervisory special agent studied the patterns in the dust along the floor. "Which way?"

"I don't know. He must've doubled back and covered his tracks." He aimed his flashlight and weapon down the right corridor. He kicked at an old crate and launched it down the tunnel. "She could be anywhere."

SSA Peters pinched the push-to-talk button on his radio and angled his chin down. "Striker, West, double back and meet us in the left tunnel." SSA Peters circled into his peripheral vision, heavy eyebrows outlining dark eyes in the flood of his flashlight beam. "You know this guy better than any of us. You're one of the best profilers I've ever worked with. You can get into his head. You can find her by knowing how he works."

"She doesn't have time. You heard her scream. That wasn't a scream for help. That was a scream from pain," Nicholas said. "He's torturing her. He's killing her, and I'm stuck here without a damn idea of how to get to her."

"Say…again… Peters?" Static broke through their comms. A gunshot exploded from the corridor behind them as the connection to Striker and West cut out.

His pulse rocketed higher. Warning lightninged through him as Nicholas turned back the way they'd come. The team was under attack, but he wasn't going to let Dr. Caldwell win this time. "The son of a bitch knows we're here. He's going to try to take us out one by one again, just as he did at the pier. He wants to lead us away from his victim in hopes of running out the clock."

Stepping into his path, SSA Peters gripped Nicholas's vest in one hand and shoved him down the right tunnel, his weapon in the other. "Do you remember what I said to you when you took this case?"

"What the hell are you doing, Peters? They need our help." Nicholas pushed against his SSA, but Peters wouldn't budge. Desperation to neutralize the threat knotted in his chest as the BAU team leader's words echoed in his head.

"I told you it isn't every day we find out the people we trust the most aren't who they seem, but what I should've said was, it isn't every day we let the people we trust show us who they really are. What Cole Presley did is unforgivable, but Aubrey Flood isn't the man who betrayed you, Nicholas. Don't let that old bastard keep you from finally being happy." SSA Peters released his hold, and Nicholas stepped back. "Go. Find Dr. Flood and get her the hell out of here. We'll handle Caldwell."

"Watch your back." Nicholas nodded. He knew who Aubrey really was. He'd known from the moment he'd met her during the X Marks the Spot Killer investigation, but his own fear of trusting the wrong person again, of not being able to see the threat coming, had shut down the possibility of something more between them. He wanted her. He wanted to trust her, to be close to her more than he'd ever wanted another human being. Cole Presley had shown him the worst mankind had to offer, but Aubrey had shown him the best, and without her, he feared he'd never let anyone get close again.

"Watch yours." SSA Peters disappeared down the corridor.

Nicholas faced two historical streets leading in

separate directions. Peters would take care of the team. He had to focus on finding Aubrey. She'd been taken down one of these passages, and from the sound of her scream, time was running out. "Which direction, Doc? Give me another hint."

The calm space he used to deep dive into the case demanded focus, and Nicholas automatically went back to that moment in Aubrey's apartment building, the one when she'd framed his face between her hands and leveled those honey-warm eyes on his. Her voice faded in and out and settled the fire burning through him. Seattle's underground phased out as the details of the investigation pushed to the front of his mind. Aubrey. He forced stillness through his body and closed his eyes. His pulse steadied, his breathing evening out.

Caldwell's compulsion to kill was a combination of pride and a need for attention. The King County medical examiner had formed an unhealthy attachment to Aubrey. The pathologist felt as though she'd taken the limelight from him. He wouldn't kill her quickly. Not unless forced, but he would want to display his handiwork when he was finished. That was why he'd used the spotlight in the slaughterhouse. There was a chance Caldwell would want to do it again, which meant he'd need electricity.

Nicholas raised his flashlight to the ceiling.

Different sizes of aluminum piping and electrical wiring ran through the rafters above. Broken light bulbs reached down from the ceiling in equidistant measurements. He wasn't looking for something as old as the shops and tunnels themselves. Caldwell would've had to upgrade the wiring to fit his needs. There. He separated a single bright orange extension cord from the darker, dust-covered collection, and followed it down the corridor to the right. Weapon aimed high, he listened for signs of movement as he searched each storefront before moving on to the next. "Come on. I know you're here somewhere."

The corridor ended ahead. There weren't any more shops to search.

He'd reached a dead end.

Nicholas lowered his flashlight and weapon but hesitated. The beam from his flashlight cut in half, one side highlighting the wall to his right, the other landing on the wall in front of him. Not a solid wall. He took a step forward, then another, before realizing the dead end wasn't the end at all. The brick turned a corner into a wall of brick that'd been disassembled. This section hadn't been noted in the blueprints West pulled from the city, but Caldwell had known about it somehow. Keeping his back to one wall, Nicholas ducked through the opening. More brick. More dust. More silence. Bright light hit him in the face, and he raised one hand to block the on-slaught to his vision.

"Is someone there?" a soft voice asked.

"Doc, is that you?" He dropped his hand, try-ing to get eyes on her. He wasn't too late. She was still alive. "Where is he? Where's Caldwell?"

"I knew you'd find me," she said.

"Aubrey?" His eyes adjusted slower than he needed them to, then he saw her. Bound in a chair, her head slumped forward as though she'd simply fallen asleep. The spotlight reflected back from a scalpel buried in her left wrist. The blade had pinned her to the chair, and she couldn't use her other arm to get free. Nicholas hol-stered his weapon and crouched in front of her. Blood. There was so much blood. Not only run-ning from her pinned wrist but from around her mouth. "Aubrey, wake up. Stay with me."

He wasn't a medical professional. He didn't know how to pull the scalpel from her wrist with-out putting her in more danger of bleeding out. "You need to tell me what to do, Doc. You have to help me get you out of here."

"Severed radial artery. Can't…pull it out." She lifted her head, those warm eyes brightening. The spotlight washed color from her features and intensified the dried blood around her mouth. "Caldwell killed… Kara. He killed Paige. He compromised the evidence, but… I have proof."

"That doesn't matter right now. I'm going to get you out of here. Okay? But first, you need to tell me how to stop you from bleeding out if I remove the scalpel," he said.

"I bit him. I swallowed…the evidence." Sweat built along her temple as she closed her eyes. She was losing consciousness. "You can prove…he did it."

Nicholas attached his flashlight to his vest and unholstered the blade at his ankle. He cut through the rope binding her wrist and both feet. "Come on, Doc. Don't give up on me now. Tell me how to stop the bleeding."

The spotlight lost power, throwing them into darkness.

"I'm afraid it's a little too late for that, Agent James." Archer Caldwell lunged.

HER FINGERS IN her left hand had gone numb.

Aubrey tried to curl them around the end of the chair's arm—to feel something, anything— but the scalpel hadn't only severed her radial artery, it'd most likely damaged the nerves in her hand.

She dragged her head over her shoulder, trying to locate Nicholas, but the spotlight had lost power. The only light came from a flashlight swinging wildly through the small area Dr. Caldwell had brought her. A fist connected with flesh and bone, and a deep growl registered through the dark. "Nicholas."

Dr. Caldwell would kill him if given the opportunity.

She had to help him. Aubrey forced her eyes open. She was losing blood for the second time in under a week. Her body had yet to recover from Dr. Caldwell's first attempt to exsanguinate her, but she couldn't leave Nicholas to fight this battle on his own. No matter what'd happened between them. He didn't deserve to die because of her. She leaned forward in the chair. The rope around her ankles and left wrist had been cut away and cracked under the weight of her feet as she straightened. The pain in her scapula and broken ribs tore a sob from her throat. The rotation in her right arm had been severely limited since her injury, but Nicholas needed her help. She wasn't going to let Archer Caldwell win.

Nicholas's scream filled the underground chamber and severed the detachment she'd forced on herself since their conversation in the observation room. Agony ripped across her back and down her right side as she cleared the rest of her forearm from the sling, and an answering sob ricocheted off the exposed brick.

"Do you hear that, Agent James? She's dying, and there's nothing you can do to stop it. No one can stop me." Dr. Caldwell's outline separated from the shadows with the help of Nicholas's flashlight strapped to his vest. He stood over Nicholas and thrust a hard kick to the profiler's rib cage. A hard exhale rushed from Nicholas's mouth, and he curled in on himself. Caldwell slammed his fist into Nicholas's face, and her partner's head snapped back against the concrete.

Nicholas went still.

"Stop. Stop it." Aubrey pressed her weight into her left elbow. Anger tore up her throat. It mixed with Dr. Caldwell's blood still coating her mouth, burning, twisting and carving her into pieces. No. She'd already lost Kara. She couldn't lose Nicholas, too. The past few days had broken her down to nothing, but Nicholas had gone out of his way to help her rebuild. He'd put her needs first, made her feel wanted. Made her feel loved. She didn't care if it'd surfaced out of the trauma she'd sustained from discovering her sister's body or nearly dying in that slaughterhouse. Her feelings were real. They mattered, and no one was going to take that away from her. Least of all a copycat killer who blamed her for his own weaknesses. "Get away from him."

She used her last ounces of strength and endurance to raise her right arm and wrap her hand around the scalpel pinning her wrist to the chair. The blade had most likely severed her radial artery. If she pulled it out without stanching the blood flow, she'd lose consciousness within thirty seconds and bleed out within two minutes.

Nicholas kicked out and shoved his attacker back into a standing tray of surgical instruments a few feet away, dislodging his flashlight in the process. The beam spun wildly across the floor then steadied on the collection of tools that'd hit the concrete. Her heart jerked in her chest as shadows consumed her partner, the fight growing more brutal, more violent. There. Dr. Caldwell's clamp had landed less than three feet away, but without the use of both hands, it'd take a miracle to reach it.

She had to try.

Blood trickled down the inside of her wrist. The only thing keeping her from bleeding out was the scalpel, but it was also what was killing her. Aubrey pressed herself out of the chair and extended her right leg. The agony in her wrist and opposite shoulder threatened to pull her back into unconsciousness, but she couldn't give up. Not until she and Nicholas were safe. Tears burned down her face as another sob broke free. She could make it. She had to make it. She slid her foot along the floor and stretched as far as her boot would reach. Her toes scraped along the side of the clamp but only managed to push it farther away. "Come on."

"You'll never lay another hand on her, you son

of a bitch." Nicholas surged off the floor and attacked with a brutalness she'd never seen in person. He slammed Dr. Caldwell back into a pillar. Once. Twice. The pathologist's groan filled the corridor as Nicholas threw a right hook, then a left.

Her eyes adjusted as the fight unfolded. Blood sprayed across the floor and up her leg, and her heart rocketed into her throat. Whether it'd come from Nicholas or Dr. Caldwell, she didn't know, but the sight of those drops pushed her harder. She had to get to the clamp, but the fact she couldn't turn her wrist with the scalpel still pinning her to the chair put it that much farther out of reach. She pointed her toes as much as her boot would let her and swept her leg across the floor. The clamp skidded closer. A burst of relieved laughter escaped up her throat, and she pulled her leg back toward her. She could almost reach the instrument. Just a few more inches. Agonizing pressure built in her fractured shoulder as she crouched and straightened her arm. The pain stole the oxygen from her lungs. The tip of her middle finger glided across the clamp's handle.

The spotlight switched back on.

She closed her eyes and turned her head away, losing contact with the instrument.

"I haven't given you enough credit, Dr. Flood.

Once again, I've underestimated your determination to ruin my plans." Dr. Caldwell swiped blood from his face with the back of a bloodied hand and stalked toward her. "You can't even die the way I want you to."

She gasped at the sight of Nicholas's prone outline across the room. He wasn't dead. She had to believe that. She had to believe Dr. Caldwell would stick to the MO and only kill his intended victim, but she wasn't an expert in profiling or psychology. She didn't know how far a killer would go to stop anyone who got in their way. It didn't matter. If she left the scalpel in her wrist, both she and Nicholas would die down here. "What did you do?"

Caldwell maneuvered around the spotlight, closing in on her. He wrapped his fingers around the scalpel and twisted the blade through her wrist. "Did you really think I was going to let him take you from me, Aubrey? How many times do I have to make my point? You did everything you could to keep me in your shadow, but now I'm the one with the power. I'm the one who is going to be remembered years from now, and you'll be nothing more than a footnote."

Her scream ricocheted inside her head, over and over, until she wasn't sure if she was still conscious. She slumped against the chair. Wood cut into her uninjured ribs, and the pain in her hand and wrist vanished. A crash of metal pierced through the haze suffocating her. The scalpel had shifted in her wrist. She was losing blood faster than before. The clamp. She needed the clamp.

"I'm not finished with you." Nicholas's voice chased back the numbness clawing up her arm and into her chest. He sounded closer. Almost within arm's reach.

"I'm not…finished with you…either." Aubrey dragged her eyes open as another crash reverberated through the room. Nicholas and Caldwell battled for dominance, each trying to physically break the other, but she only had attention for the clamp. Reaching down, she didn't even feel the pain in her shoulder and wrapped her fingers around the stainless-steel instrument. She pressed her elbow against the chair and hauled herself off the floor. Blood pulsed out of her wrist, every second draining precious milliliters she couldn't afford to lose. She set the clamp on her lap and gripped the scalpel. She had less than thirty seconds to secure the clamp before she lost consciousness and never woke up. Shadows shifted in her peripheral vision, the ringing in her ears too loud.

She pulled the scalpel from her wrist.

Blood gushed from the wound and soaked the grain of the wooden chair and her slacks.

The blade fell from her hand, the tang of metal against concrete barely registering as she grasped the clamp. She didn't have time to ensure it'd been sterilized. If she lived through this—if she and Nicholas made it out of here—the hospital could take care of any infection. Aubrey struggled to keep her eyes open as she inserted the clamp into the wound. The pain was gone now. There was only survival. She compressed the clamp's teeth where she believed Caldwell had lacerated her artery, and an instant exhaustion flooded through her. The bleeding slowed, but the longer the clamp obstructed blood flow to her hand, the higher chance she'd never be able to use it again.

Reality came into focus with measured breaths, and she caught sight of Nicholas. Her partner struggled to free himself from the pinning grip of Dr. Caldwell's hands around his throat. If the pathologist pressed down with too much force, he'd crush the profiler's larynx and the man she loved would suffocate in a matter of minutes.

The man she loved.

Aubrey slid from the chair, wrapping her hand around the scalpel she'd pulled from her wrist. The fractures in her shoulder had taken a considerable amount of strength from her grip, but she wouldn't need much. The best medical examiners made the best killers.

Caldwell had turned his back toward her. Nicholas's feet pressed into the floor to unbalance his attacker, but it wasn't enough. Those green-blue eyes she'd come to rely on widened as she arced the scalpel down and stabbed the blade through the occipital nerves at the base of Dr. Caldwell's skull.

The pathologist's body went rigid, and his hands fell from around Nicholas's neck. Faster than her blood-deprived brain registered, Nicholas rolled his attacker to the floor. His gaze dipped to her wrist, to the clamp hanging from the wound, then raised to her. "Aubrey, are you—"

The strength in her legs failed.

He caught her as she collapsed. Staring down at her, Nicholas swept her hair out of her face as he positioned her across his lap. Shouts echoed down the corridors and tunnels, but he never left her. "In here! Call an ambulance!" He hauled her closer, setting his forehead against hers. "I've got you, Doc. I've got you."

She closed her eyes, reveling in the warmth his body injected as the cold crept in. She tried to thread her hands through his hair, but her extremities wouldn't respond. "Have I ever told you…your hair…is as pretty as a periwinkle… flower on a pony?"

"Aubrey, come on," he said. "Stay with me."

She wanted to, but the blackness pulled her under.

Chapter Fifteen

Archer Caldwell was dead.

The damage Aubrey had done to the occipital nerves at the back of his neck had instantly killed him, but the damage the son of a bitch had caused over the past few days would last for years.

Nicholas refreshed the glass of water on the side table beside the hospital bed and took a seat. Remote in hand, he turned on the TV and switched the channels until he found Aubrey's favorite show. The one with the toy doctor who could bring her stuffed animals to life. Monitors punctuated each beat of her heart as she slept.

The surgeons had been able to suture the severed artery in her wrist, but the amount of trauma she'd been through in the slaughterhouse, combined with the damage to her wrist two days ago, had forced her doctor to sedate Aubrey in order to speed her recovery.

"All right, the little girl with a magical stethoscope is having a hard time after making a big mistake at her clinic. She's wondering if her patients would be better off if she hadn't been there at all, but I think we both know how this one is going to end," he said. "Hell, you've probably watched it half a dozen times yourself, but I've got to tell you, I feel kind of bad for her."

Three quick knocks punctured the bubble he'd created inside the small room since she'd been released from surgery. The door swung open, and Dashiell West nodded. "How's she doing today?"

Nicholas turned off the television and set the remote on the side table near Aubrey's glass of water. "Her doctors came in about an hour ago to take her off the sedation meds. Her vitals are steady, but it's taking a while for her to wake up. They tell me it's nothing to worry about for now. If everything goes well, she'll be awake soon." He sat higher in the chair. "What's up?"

"Figured you'd want an update on the Caldwell investigation." West closed the door behind him softly and took the chair closest to the door. "Caitlyn has been keeping the families in the loop. The new medical examiner finished his re-examination of Kara Flood's and Paige Cress's remains and has released both victims to their families for final arrangements."

"That's good. You were there while he did the examination?" Nicholas studied Aubrey's sleeping form, her dark brown hair framing her face. The fractured shoulder blade, two broken ribs and the scalpel in her wrist hadn't stopped her from saving his life down in those tunnels. He'd see this through to the end. For her.

"Yeah. Seemed Caldwell went out of his way to make sure the evidence he recovered from both victims wouldn't tie back to him, but from what the new ME said, it's pretty clear who attacked Kara Flood and Paige Cress. The cast the pathologist made of Paige's teeth matches the wound on Caldwell's forearm, and the lab recovered epithelial cells from the dog's leash used to strangle Kara. He wore gloves, but the doc's sister must've struggled enough to scrape one edge of the leash against her attacker's neck. There are faint scratches under Caldwell's jaw."

West motioned toward Aubrey. "On top of that, the blood Aubrey swallowed after she bit Caldwell came back as a DNA match for the tissue the ME's assistant pulled from between Paige Cress's teeth. He tried to contaminate the sample, but the solution he'd used breaks down DNA over time. We caught it before there was too much damage. Forensics wasn't able to pull prints from the map he taped to Dr. Flood's door or from the Polaroid Caldwell left with the dog, but the shoe print outside Kara Flood's apartment is a perfect match and size to a pair of boots from

Caldwell's apartment. Soil samples confirm he was there, and CSU found three bottles of perfume with both victims' fingerprints and Dr. Flood's on the glass from his bathroom. Looks like the bastard was collecting trophies from his kills. You'll also be happy to know Dyson found a regular from AfterDark who was willing to sit down with one of our composite artists. She described all four book club members to a tee."

"You should've seen her." Nicholas couldn't keep the admiration out of his voice. Even in the face of death, Aubrey had stood up against her attacker and killed him before the bastard could kill Nicholas. No matter how many times he found himself in awe of her determination and self-sacrifice, she surprised him. "Anything else?"

"I decrypted Dr. Caldwell's personal laptop drive. I found these." West handed over the file in his hand, and Nicholas forced himself to tear his gaze from Aubrey to take it. "Surveillance photos. Caldwell might've tampered with the evidence tying him to Kara Flood's and Paige Cress's murders, but he didn't get rid of all of it. Seems I can break a serial killer's encryption, but proving my sister's innocence is beyond my capabilities."

West's sister. Arrested for embezzling funds from the investment bank where she worked as a hedge fund manager. Nicholas understood the obsession to protect the people he cared about and to use the very justice system he believed in to do it, but sometimes the law was out of their hands. He flipped through dozens of photos obviously taken with a telephoto lens. Kara Flood walking her dog, Koko, down the same section of sidewalk where she'd been found dead. Paige Cress outside her employer's office. Aubrey in one of Harborview Medical's hospital wings. He hesitated, his thumb tracing over the curve of her jaw in the photo, and lifted his gaze to the warm, real-life woman in the hospital bed.

He'd been wrong about her after Simon Curry's interrogation. He'd accused her of using the trauma she'd been through to cling to the next person who'd shown her any kind of attention, but the truth was, it'd probably taken everything she had to trust him with her safety and welfare. Aubrey had spent nearly her entire life putting others first, always ignoring her own needs in the hope the love she showed would be returned, and he'd thrown it in her face. He'd accused her of weakness when, in fact, she was the strongest woman he'd ever met in his life. Once again, if it hadn't been for her, Nicholas wouldn't have made it out of the underground.

He closed the file and handed it back to West. "We have proof that ties Caldwell to each of the victims. It'll be enough to close the case and give the families the closure they deserve. Great work, West. We got him."

"Thought you'd be a little more enthusiastic about it." West pushed to his feet, his gaze shifting to Aubrey. "But I imagine you've got other things on your mind." The cybercrimes expert half saluted toward the hospital bed with the file folder. "Looks like she's coming around. I'll give you two some time."

The monitor on the other side of the bed ticked up in rhythm, and Nicholas shoved to his feet. The hospital room door clicked closed behind him as West exited. Sliding his hand beneath hers, he studied the subtle changes in Aubrey's expression as she battled to open her eyes. "Hey, Doc."

"Hey." She focused on him, and the world righted itself in an instant. Her tongue darted across her bottom lip as she scanned the room, took in the machines tracking her vitals, then came back to him. Her gaze dipped to the cast around her left hand, and his heart jerked in his chest. Aubrey Flood was—had been—one of the best pathologists in the country, and the tears welling in her eyes told him she knew exactly what the extensive damage to her wrist meant. "I can't feel my fingers. Nerve damage?"

Nicholas massaged his thumb into her forearm above the cast, but no amount of physical or verbal comfort would change what'd happened. "Yeah, Doc. Your surgeon did everything he could, but the damage Caldwell caused… They said there's still a chance of making a full recovery with physical therapy and time, but—"

"But I won't be able to hold a scalpel again. I won't be able to keep my job or help the people who've lost their loved ones find answers." Her voice deadpanned, her expression as neutral as her words. She pulled her hand away from his and set her forearm across her eyes. "Even dead, Dr. Caldwell got exactly what he wanted."

"I'm fairly certain he wanted to walk out of those tunnels alive. You made sure that didn't happen. You made sure he couldn't hurt anyone ever again." Nicholas brought his chair closer and took a seat. Tugging her hand back into his, he swept the tear that'd escaped from one eye away with his thumb. He had to be sure. He had to be sure this wasn't a dream, that she was alive, that she was really here, but hell, even if it wasn't real, he'd do whatever it took not to wake up.

"You saved my life. And my team's lives, Aubrey. You made sure we all got out of there alive. You might not be able to hold a scalpel again, but there are plenty of ways you can still help the people who need you. You're stronger than you think. No matter how many times you get knocked down, you stand back up. That's what I love about you."

Her gaze cut to his, confusion swirling through the honey depths. "What do you mean, that's what you love about me?"

"I mean I was an idiot." He shook his head, a humorless laugh filling the tension between them as their last conversation replayed in his head for the hundredth—or was it the thousandth?—time. "After Simon Curry's interrogation, I discounted your instincts about his innocence and blamed your attachment to me on the trauma you'd been through in the slaughterhouse. We had a perfectly viable suspect on the other side of that glass, but I was wrong, and I was wrong to invalidate your feelings. I didn't give you enough credit. I should've known after what you'd been through you were stronger than that, but the truth is, I was scared."

"It's hard to believe anything scares you," she said.

"Cole Presley made me believe he was a good man. Hell, he helped raise me and my sister. He took care of my mom when she didn't have anyone else to rely on, and he manipulated me into thinking he cared about us. But after the truth came out, I swore I wouldn't ever let someone manipulate me like that again."

Nicholas studied the fine lines of the sling on

her right arm, heat rising up his throat. "Then you came along, and when you told me you'd finally found someone you didn't have to hide your true self with, I convinced myself you were manipulating me as he had. I convinced myself that you were wearing a mask to get what you needed from me before you left."

SHE DIDN'T KNOW what to say, what to think.

Nicholas had been through one of the worst betrayals a person could experience when Cole Presley had revealed who he was behind that friendly neighbor/father-figure mask, and her chest hurt witnessing the pain in his voice now, but she needed to know. She needed to know how they could move on from this. Because even though he'd crushed her heart in that observation room, a part of her still stood by what she'd said. She didn't have to hide pieces of herself from him. She didn't have to convince him she was a pediatrician or explain her need to autopsy human beings to give comfort to their loved ones. She didn't have to hide the fact she'd rather watch a silly children's show instead of the news or a true crime documentary or listen to a podcast all her colleagues and friends had become obsessed with.

"Do you blame me for being the one to prove Cole Presley was the X Marks the Spot Killer?"

Aubrey willed her fingers to curl around his, but the signals from her brain had died the moment Dr. Caldwell had stabbed that scalpel through her wrist. The hollowness of facing the fact she'd never hold a surgical instrument steadily again had cut through her, but worse, the fear Nicholas would never be able to trust her hooked into her and pulled tight. "Do you resent me because you think I made a mistake on that case?"

The three distinct lines between his eyebrows deepened in confusion. He shifted to the edge of his seat and locked both hands around her cast. The dark circles under his eyes evidenced his lack of sleep, and it was only then she realized he'd slept in the clothes he was wearing. He'd stayed here. With her. "What? No. You did your job, Doc, and you're damn good at it. The evidence proved he killed all those women. You proved it. You're the one who showed the world who he really was, and I could never blame you for that."

"But you won't ever trust me." The pain of that statement sliced deeper than the fractures to her ribs and scapula. She'd trusted him. She'd trusted him to find her when Caldwell had abducted her from the pier, and afterward when he'd promised he wouldn't let anything else happen to her. She'd trusted him with pieces of her and Kara's childhood and to find the man responsible for murdering her sister. She'd trusted him with her heart, even at the risk of not being wanted in return. Tightness swelled in her throat.

"All I've done is trust you during this investigation, Nicholas. You made me feel wanted and worthy when you watched my favorite show with me and made doughnuts for me. When you held me and let me cry in your arms, I felt…loved. You showed me I was burning out by putting others first, but when I finally made myself a priority by telling you I didn't want to hide any part of myself from you, you reduced my feelings to an effect from trauma. It might not seem like much, but it took everything I had to convince myself what I felt was real—that I deserved to be happy—and it meant nothing to you. I am not Cole Presley, Agent James. That man manipulated and lied to you for thirty years, but there isn't an ounce of blood in my body that could do that to someone I love."

Seconds slipped by, a minute.

"You don't exactly know whose blood you have in your body now, but you're right, Doc. About all of it." Nicholas sat back as though she'd thrown a physical blow. He released her hand, and she swore the dead nerves in her fingertips went cold. Standing, he cast his gaze to the floor. "What I did had nothing to do with you and everything to do with fear of trusting someone who could hurt me again, and I'm sorry. I was falling in love with you, and losing control of myself like that scared the hell out of me. You're nothing like Cole Presley. I know the person I've spent the past week with on this investigation is who you really are, and I stupidly took it for granted. You're generous and sincere—a bit macabre, considering you used to make Kara play dead as a kid—but it took nearly losing you for me to realize you are everything I've been afraid of and everything I've needed in my life."

He pushed unkempt hair off his forehead and hauled a duffel bag she hadn't noticed until now from the floor over his shoulder. The stitches in the right side of his face shifted as one side of his mouth curled into a half smile. "I wouldn't blame you if you never wanted to see me after I leave this room, but you deserved an explanation."

Nicholas headed for the door.

Her heart rate ticked higher on the monitors as she struggled to sit straight in the bed. "You were falling in love with me?"

He hesitated, his hand on the door handle, every ounce the BAU agent she'd fallen in love with. Intense, focused, protective. Craning his head toward her, he tightened his grip around the bag's strap until the whites of his knuckles materialized through bruised and lacerated skin. "I started falling in love with you the first time

I met you, Doc. I just didn't realize it until I almost lost you to Caldwell in that slaughterhouse."

Heat exploded under her rib cage as time distorted into a comforting fluid, and she recalled their first meeting in the morgue at Harborview Medical Center. They'd met during an autopsy of one of the X Marks the Spot Killer's victims, and while she didn't exactly consider that a story worth telling to friends and family, she couldn't discount that case had started her on a path she'd never regret taking. Not when it'd led to him, to this moment. "Even surrounded by all those dead bodies?"

Nicholas unshouldered his overnight bag and dropped it into a chair by the door. A laugh rumbled through him, and those green-blue eyes brightened as he turned to face her. "You're a medical examiner. It would've been weird if there hadn't been any dead bodies."

"Well, isn't that sweeter than a sugar cookie in the supermarket?" She couldn't help but smile as she nodded toward the edge of the hospital bed, and he took her direction, sitting again. The mattress dipped under his weight, anchoring her to the moment. "In case it wasn't obvious, I love you, too."

"Does that mean you forgive me?" His smile notched her awareness of him higher just before he leaned into her, careful of her wrist, and pressed his mouth to hers.

She set her head back against the pillows. "Get me some real, unburned chocolate doughnuts with rainbow sprinkles and rescue Koko from Animal Services, and I might consider it."

"Anything for you, Doc," he said.

Hints of his aftershave chased back the antiseptic smell she'd become accustomed to over the years. She hadn't realized how much she'd come to rely on that smell, that it'd become part of her. Her smile faltered as she examined the cast. She wouldn't know the extent of her injury until she was able to discuss her diagnosis with her surgeon herself, but something deep inside said whatever came next, she and Nicholas would handle it. Together.

She tried to curl her fingers into her palm, but the tendons in her wrist needed a considerable time to recover. "It's really over, isn't it? I didn't imagine it."

"Caldwell can't hurt you anymore." He smoothed his thumb over the back of her arm, and the nightmares hiding behind her eyes seemed like a distant memory. The violent lacerations along the side of his face transformed the profiler into a rougher version of himself, one she couldn't seem to pull away from. "He can't hurt anyone. The new county medical examiner released Kara's and Paige's remains to the families. He was able to prove Archer Caldwell attacked both victims after you took a bite out of him and preserved his DNA. They're going home because of you, Aubrey. Once you've been discharged, we can put this whole thing behind us."

"Then what? What am I supposed to do if I can't be down in that morgue to give families the answers they're looking for?" How did she not let Caldwell win?

"You'll figure it out. You just need to take it one day at a time and know you're not alone. It's going to take time. You're going to want to give up, and it's going to be painful, but I'll be there with you every step of the way. As long as we're together, we can get through anything."

Nicholas swept his fingertips across her forehead. Bending at the waist, he reached down into his duffel bag and produced a white rectangular box. "Until then, we're going to watch every episode of your favorite cartoon and make ourselves sick with these."

Her mouth watered as he revealed the chocolate doughnuts with her favorite multicolored sprinkles, and a laugh bubbled up through her. He'd brought her doughnuts, and she found herself falling a little bit more in love with him. The grumpy profiler she'd called in a favor to be assigned to her sister's investigation had a soft spot after all.

Aubrey used his help to straighten and crushed her mouth to his. Her profiler. Her partner. Her everything. "You realize you're going to have to feed those—and everything else—to me for the foreseeable future, right? I have to warn you, the last man who put his hand near my mouth paid the price. Are you sure you're up for such a dangerous assignment, Agent James?"

Nicholas raised a doughnut between them and set it against her lips, his smile wider than she'd ever seen it before. "I've got to tell you that makes me happier than a dead pig in sunshine, Dr. Flood."

"I don't know what that means," she said.

He kissed her again, sweeping doughnut crumbs from her mouth. "Neither do I."

Epilogue

One week later...

The pop of the cork exploded in his ears.

Shouts and claps filled the BAU conference room as Nicholas accepted the first glass of champagne from SSA Peters. It was over. The case was closed, and he couldn't help but celebrate the end of one of the most grueling, complicated cases of his career. Or that he'd walked away with the greatest prize he could've ever imagined—his future.

Aubrey flashed a wide smile up at him from her seat.

SSA Peters raised his glass, dark eyes brighter than Nicholas had seen them in a long time. "You might've cut it a bit close, Nicholas, but the FBI has officially closed the investigation into the deaths of Kara Flood and Paige Cress." He directed his attention to Aubrey.

"Dr. Flood, Director Branson has asked me

to share her condolences. While it's impossible for us to ease your grief, I wanted you to know the BAU is here for you, and it's been a privilege working alongside you. To Nicholas James and Aubrey Flood."

Aubrey gripped her glass with the tips of her fingers and raised it as high as she could. Unable to mix alcohol with her pain medication, she'd chosen to stick with water for celebratory drinks with the team.

Madeline Striker, Dashiell West, Liam McDare and David Dyson all raised their glasses in tandem. "To Nicholas and Aubrey!"

"To Nicholas," Aubrey said. "The best partner I could ask for."

Nicholas took a gulp of his champagne, one hand on her uninjured shoulder, while the team dissolved into casual conversation. He caught sight of Liam McDare as the IT expert peeled from the mass of agents, answering his phone. Tension bled into the back of Liam's neck. Angry whispers cut through the echo of conversation from the tech guru's position by the floor-to-ceiling windows overlooking Puget Sound, and Nicholas closed the distance between them.

"No, Lorelai. You know I don't want them there. I told you that before we started all this planning." Liam ended the call, his rough exhale fogging the window. He turned back to join the party but pulled up short at the sight of Nicholas. Shock quickly transformed to faked enthusiasm, but Liam refused to meet his gaze. "Congratulations on closing your case, Agent James. I've read your report. It's amazing what you did out there."

"Thanks," Nicholas said. "Everything okay? And before you lie to me, I heard some of your conversation."

Liam shook off Nicholas's concern. "It's nothing. Lorelai is traveling with the director. We haven't seen each other in a few weeks, and it's starting to show. That's all."

"She wants you to invite your parents to the wedding." Because that was what most couples were supposed to do, share their wedding day with their loved ones, family and friends, but Liam McDare and his fiancée weren't most couples. They were members of the Behavioral Analysis Unit. Every emotion, every fear was amplified ten times because of the work they dealt with day-to-day. He had firsthand experience.

"She's trying to convince me I'll regret it if I don't invite them, but she doesn't understand," Liam said. "Her parents aren't on their third spouses. They've been married over twenty years and still laugh and love each other. Mine will go at each other's throats the minute they're in the same room together."

The tech expert swung his glass out to his side. "I don't know. Sometimes I think Lorelai is more excited about the wedding than what comes afterward, and then where will we be?" He took a swig of champagne. "Right where my parents are. Miserable, divorced and bitter."

Nicholas glanced at Aubrey as she talked with West. Honey-warm eyes lightened as she turned her attention to him at the same moment, as though she'd sensed the weight of his gaze. A flood of appreciation rushed through his veins as the future spread out in front of him. The injuries to her shoulder, ribs and wrist had threatened her career, but Nicholas had known the moment he'd found her in those underground tunnels, there wasn't anything he wouldn't do to give her the life she deserved. He turned back to Liam, slapping him on the shoulder with his free hand.

"Love isn't about who's coming or not coming to the wedding, color palettes, flower choices and bridesmaids' dresses, Liam. It's about the two of you. That's all that matters. It's about trust. It's about believing that even if you don't know what comes next, you do it together, and you support one another unconditionally. That's the only way this is going to work. Talk to Lorelai. Tell her the real reason you don't want your parents at the wedding. Everything will work out."

He slipped away from Liam and stepped into Aubrey's side. He wound one arm around her waist. Pressing his mouth to her ear, he inhaled as much of her simple perfume as his lungs allowed. "Time to go, Doc. You're going to be late for your appointment."

"Appointment?" Aubrey waved to West then allowed him to drag her toward the door, confusion contorting her expression. "My appointment with the hospital administrator isn't until next week."

"Not that kind of appointment." He led her through the BAU offices and into the lobby. "This one involves sweatpants, doughnuts and cartoons, and we've got all the time in the world."

"I like the sound of that." Aubrey punched the button for the elevators. "As long as you're not making the doughnuts, that is."

He couldn't help but laugh. "Picked up an unhealthy amount from the bakery just this morning."

The elevator doors opened, but Aubrey turned into him instead of stepping into the car. Her cast scratched at his jaw as she framed his face. She pressed her mouth to his. "Well, aren't you sweeter than a porcupine eating a pineapple. I could get used to this, Agent James."

"Good." He let the elevator doors close. "Because it's only going to get better from here."

And he couldn't wait to get started.

* * * * *

*Don't miss the next books in the
Behavioral Analysis Unit series:*

Decoding a Criminal, *Barb Han,*
August 2021
Tracing a Kidnapper, *Juno Rushdan,*
September 2021
Trapping a Terrorist, *Caridad Piñeiro,*
October 2021

*Look for them when they go on sale wherever
Harlequin Intrigue books are sold!*

Get 4 FREE REWARDS!

We'll send you 2 FREE Books plus 2 FREE Mystery Gifts.

Harlequin Presents books feature the glamorous lives of royals and billionaires in a world of exotic locations, where passion knows no bounds.

FREE Value Over $20

HARLEQUIN SELECTS COLLECTION

19 FREE BOOKS IN ALL!

RaeAnne Thayne — A COLD CREEK HOMECOMING

LINDA LAEL MILLER — SIERRA'S HOMECOMING

B.J. DANIELS — MOUNTAIN SHERIFF

From Robyn Carr to RaeAnne Thayne to Linda Lael Miller and Sherryl Woods we promise (actually, GUARANTEE!) each author in the Harlequin Selects collection has seen their name on the *New York Times* or *USA TODAY* bestseller lists!
